MW01689073

She knew him now,

knew the way he had of seeming to be always underfoot, yet never in her way. She knew his penchant for sandwiches with lots of lettuce and the way he turned down his wool socks, just once, under his Levi's. She knew his crazy curiosity, that might and often did lead him in any direction.

But most of all, she'd seen that look of deep hunger pass through his eyes like a winter storm, only to move off, leaving him snowbound, unreachable. The fiercer the storm, the farther he moved, and the more she knew she wanted to draw him close, touch him, warm him.

And she knew he was a flyer. Here today and gone tomorrow. She heard the memory of her childhood, felt the pain. But she wanted him. No matter what it would take.

Dear Reader,

Welcome to Silhouette. Experience the magic of the wonderful world where two people fall in love. Meet heroines who will make you cheer for their happiness, and heroes (be they the boy next door or a handsome, mysterious stranger) who will win your heart. Silhouette Romances reflect the magic of love—sweeping you away with books that will make you laugh and cry, heartwarming, poignant stories that will move you time and time again.

In the next few months, we're publishing romances by many of your all-time favorites, such as Diana Palmer, Brittany Young, Emilie Richards and Arlene James. Your response to these authors and other authors of Silhouette Romances has served as a touchstone for us, and we're pleased to bring you more books with Silhouette's distinctive medley of charm, wit and—above all—*romance*.

I hope you enjoy this book and the many stories to come. Experience the magic!

Sincerely,

Tara Hughes
Senior Editor
Silhouette Books

CAROLYN SEABAUGH

Butterfly Autumn

Silhouette Romance

Published by Silhouette Books New York

America's Publisher of Contemporary Romance

For Mother and Dad,
who first taught me
that home is truly where the heart is

SILHOUETTE BOOKS
300 E. 42nd St., New York, N.Y. 10017

ISBN: 0-373-08468-4

First Silhouette Books printing November 1986

Printed in the U.S.A.

CAROLYN SEABAUGH

was born in Seattle, but has lived just about everywhere else since. "The Colorado Rockies, the green hills of Oklahoma, the smell of oregano growing wild on the Texas plateaus, the wildflowers of Alaska's spring...I miss them all!" Home is now Washington, D.C., and nearby Harpers Ferry, West Virginia, where she often goes to rest, write and reflect on the sense of place and its importance to the human spirit.

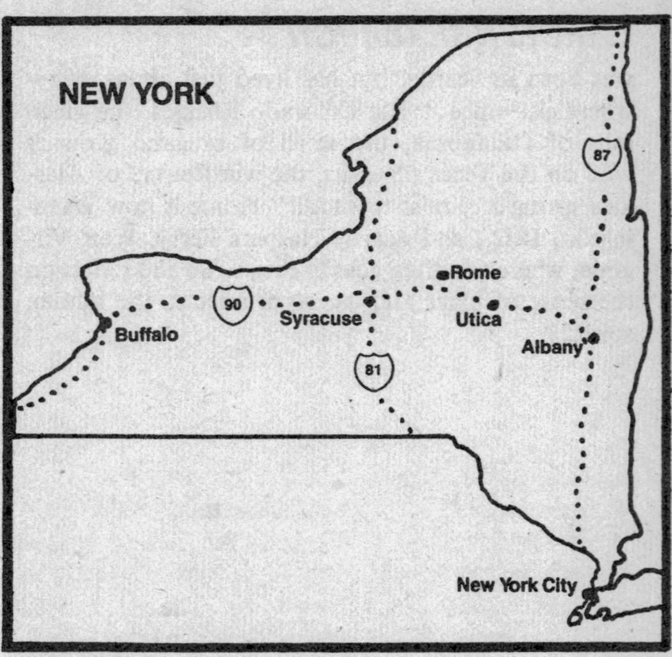
NEW YORK
87
Rome
90
Syracuse
Utica
Buffalo
Albany
81
New York City

Chapter One

Adriana tilted the worn felt visor over the upper windshield, searching for an angle that would shield her eyes against the late afternoon sun. She slowed the ancient Volkswagen, shifted down into second gear and approached the one-lane bridge. The car bumped noisily across it and labored up the steep hill beyond.

The trees were thicker here. Their density softened and all but absorbed the chugging sound of the engine. Only the sumacs hinted at fall. Reaching out amid the still green boughs of maple, oak and birch, their slipper-shaped leaves tapped on the faded green sides of the car like crimson patent leather dancing shoes. Adriana smiled, delighted that another, dependably magnificent, central New York State autumn was on its way.

She inhaled deeply the pungent odor of drying leaves, cooling pine and fading goldenrod. And then she hung her arm out the open window, trailing fingers in the rushing breeze, testing it for autumn's telltale chill.

She barely felt the velvety brush of the butterfly's wing as it hovered near her hand. For one precarious moment the bright jewel of an insect perched on her finger and clung tightly, its tattered wings splayed against her hand like some elaborate antique dinner ring. Then it was swept away. Suddenly the air was thick with butterflies—a burnished orange crescendo of fragile energy. Adriana braked as several of the insects fluttered against her windshield.

Carefully she eased her car onto the shoulder of the narrow country road, switched off the engine and climbed out. In the hush that followed, Adriana felt the air tremble with the silent whispers of a thousand delicate wings. Wave upon wave of golden monarch butterflies rose from the field at the crest of the hill, wafted by her and disappeared into the trees across the road. And with each wave a few of them fell, like painted autumn leaves, and littered the ground at her feet.

Lost in thought, she barely heard the rattletrap truck as it crossed the bridge below and climbed the hill. At last she turned, stepping back to let it pass. The battered Chevy pickup slowed, its loosely attached front bumper banging against the washed-out red frame with annoying regularity.

The driver braked when he saw her and swung wide. The breeze from his passing truck caused her car to rock slightly and she thought, for some reason, of two old lovers on a park bench in autumn oblivious to each other's shabby appearance.

The face of the man seemed to pass before her in slow motion, surveying her with polite but thorough appreciation. Adriana caught a glimpse of sandy-colored hair clipped close around a ruddy face. She could not repress a quick smile in response to his broad grin. Then she quickly lowered her eyes and crouched toward the butterflies at her feet.

She heard him stop, back up, then switch off the noisy engine. The authoritative sound of his boots, crunching the roadside gravel, quickly closed the narrow space between them.

His voice swept over her, light, quick, familiar as the countryside she'd grown to love. "Have trouble with your car, ma'am? Can I help?"

She stood, slowly smoothing a long strand of auburn hair back from one temple. She saw him watch the motion with studied interest, following the bend of her wrist, lingering on the curve of her ear as though memorizing something profoundly important. She'd seen her students look just that way midway into reading Tolkien's *Lord of the Rings*.

His absorption gave her a moment to study him. No, it wasn't just the light; there definitely was a copper tint in his sandy hair. And yes, she'd seen correctly—a scattering of boyish freckles peppered the high cheekbones and aquiline nose just beneath his mellowing summer suntan. Adriana lingered on the laugh lines that crinkled at his temples. In that moment, his cinnamon-colored eyes, surprisingly gentle, connected with hers, startling her with their intimacy.

"I stopped to watch the butterflies," she said haltingly. "I've never seen so many in one place."

She turned, discreetly increased the distance between them by a step and raised an arm to shade her eyes as she looked uphill toward the open field. But her action only served to rivet his attention. She felt his appreciative gaze take in her profile, slip down the thin gauze of her white, snug-fitting shirt and linger where she knew it stretched too tightly across her full breasts. Quickly she lowered her arm and shoved her hands into the pockets of her faded blue cords.

"This must be a resting place on their migratory route." She felt her gaze drawn upward by the comfortable familiarity of his voice. Arms crossed casually over a blue chambray shirt, he nodded with authority toward the woods across the road. "They're probably roosting in the trees over there."

"Roosting?" Adriana tested the sound of the word, found it incongruous and said so.

He shrugged. "That's what they call it," he said. "Let's check it out." Without waiting for her acceptance, he took her elbow firmly, steered her across the road and guided her down a narrow footpath that bent back into thick woods. His secure grip seemed to command obedience. Adriana fought against her own subtle desire to submit and tried to think of some unobtrusive way to turn back to the safety of the road. Suddenly he stopped and nodded toward the trees ahead.

She felt her breath catch as his grip tightened momentarily. When she inhaled again, it was the deep rich scent of the man beside her, musk mixed with a woodsy smell, heady yet somehow comforting. "I don't see a thing," Adriana whispered. At the sound of her quavering voice, what had looked like a cluster of dry leaves on a bent branch trembled and unfolded. Half a dozen sets of orange-gold monarch wings opened in a stray sliver of sunlight.

"I see them now," she whispered excitedly. "I never knew their wings were creamy colored underneath."

He laughed gently, slid his hand easily into her own, raised it and pointed to the clusters of roosting butterflies. The action seemed natural, unassuming. Adriana felt her hand grow warm in his. "It's excellent camouflage," he said, indicating the closed wings. "They'll stay that way all night until the air warms enough for them to spread their wings and move on."

"Speaking of moving on," she said, gently disengaging her hand, "I have an errand and it's getting late."

He did not protest or try to touch her again as she half expected he might, but followed her back up the path at some distance. She paused before she crossed the road, noting that the VW was deteriorating rapidly; even next to that ramshackle red pickup it looked positively shabby. Maybe Calvin was right. She really ought to replace it with a more respectable car.

As she reached for the door handle, one last wave of butterflies rose from the field above, scattering a foamy trail of milkweed seeds in its wake. She turned to watch them disappear into the woods beyond, over the head of the man about to cross the road to join her. He, too, stopped to watch.

She saw then the massive build of his straight, trimly tapered back and shoulders. He was not a large man; still, she guessed that the worn chambray shirt, stretched tautly over his large biceps, hid incredible strength. Her eyes moved irresistibly past the shirt, tucked neatly into the faded denims, past the wide leather belt. As her eyes traveled downward, she felt her pulse quicken and tease her imagination unmercifully. Clenching her fist against the lingering feeling of his touch on her palm, she thought, *I must have been crazy to go into the woods with that man.* Wide-eyed, she watched him turn again and move toward her.

Adriana felt rooted to the ground as he strode across the road. He stopped so close to her that she could feel the warmth of his breath on her upturned face. "Hold still," he commanded.

Adriana froze, heart pounding. Eyes straight ahead, she focused on the coppery shadow at his angular, unshaven jawline. She felt him reach into her hair and catch up a strand and then a huge monarch butterfly lay cradled in his palm. Her breath exploded in a sigh of released tension that nearly swept the insect from his hand. In his sharp glance, she watched a question form. Adriana looked into the brown-gold eyes and thought of the butterflies asleep in the woods beyond. Would they all end as this one?

"At least she doesn't have to make the trip," he said. "Looks like she's been through quite a lot already." He traced the edge of a tattered wing.

Adriana watched the question return to his eyes and skirted it. "How do you know it's a female?" she asked.

"See how she's missing the little black scent spot on each hind wing?" His voice took on an inquisitive brightness that caught her interest. "She was probably born here last summer," he continued. "She flew south to winter, maybe as far as a thousand miles, then returned to the milkweed field to lay her eggs. With around four hundred per female, it's likely that some of her children are roosting in those woods we visited." He hesitated, his brown eyes deepening in the gathering shadows.

"You're right," she said. "She's been through quite a lot." A sudden gust of wind caught the butterfly and lifted it out of his hands. They watched it fall some distance away, hardly distinguishable from the yellow leaves that littered the roadside. He did not move away from her but stood, his eyes fastened on her own. She saw the questioning look deepen, become some distant troubled hunger.

"How do you happen to know so much about monarch butterflies?" she ventured lightly, trying to put verbal if not physical distance between them.

The easy grin returned. "Science project in grade school," he answered. "Our class tagged butterflies for a study out of the University of Toronto. Wish I knew how it ended."

"Ended?" she asked.

"Yes." His answer was tinged with a singular mixture of humor and regret. "Unfortunately we moved before the spring."

Adriana started at the comment. For all the world he looked as if he'd always been a part of the central New York countryside. "I really did want to stay and see if any of those butterflies made it back," he continued. "You don't happen to remember seeing any monarchs with small red gummed tags during the summer of sixty-one, do you?"

"No," she said and laughed. "I don't even remember where *I* was during the summer of sixty-one."

"Then you're not from around here?" The question hung in the air. It was the same one she'd wanted to ask him.

"Oh, yes." She said the words emphatically. "I am most certainly from around here! For good. Forever. I've moved enough in my life to know that I'll *never* do it again."

Her words rang in the still air between them, their note of resolution some sort of signal to which he responded by opening the door of her car for her. She slid inside.

"You'd really be great at butterfly tagging," he said as he closed the door. "I've heard they need people who stay put."

"Maybe I'll look into it," she replied matter-of-factly, choosing to respond to the comment and not to the laugh lines that deepened around his mischievous eyes. She sighed with relief as she always did when the small engine finally turned over.

Now it was his turn to step aside as she moved out onto the road, swung around his truck and headed up the hill. The last of the late afternoon sunlight bounced off the old red Chevy pickup to settle, glinting, in his copper-blond hair. Adriana resisted the urge to watch his figure disappear in her rearview mirror. She accelerated and crested the hill.

She had put five miles between them, but still his image lingered in her mind. He was not handsome in the traditional way, she decided, but those expressive brown-gold eyes and that boyish grin were, well, definitely engaging. And his hair invited touching. Adriana tossed her own long auburn hair impatiently off her shoulders, pushed the visor back out of the way and glanced again at the newspaper ad on the seat beside her. She forced her concentration to the roadside mailboxes, searching for the name mentioned in the ad.

Finally she braked and pulled the VW off onto a deeply rutted farm road. She wound around two sharp bends and circled a neat white clapboard farmhouse, freshly painted. Beyond the house, a graveled parking area bordered by lavish yellow chrysanthemums sported a huge satellite dish in its center. Adriana pulled the VW up beside the dish and shut off the ignition. Almost immediately she heard the unmistakable clatter of the pickup.

Calvin would say *I told you so*. He'd warned her, on more than one occasion, not to talk to strangers. She'd always protested. What's the use of living in a small town? she'd said. If she stuck to his old-fashioned rules she'd never meet a soul. Except she'd censored "old-fashioned." Calvin hated to be reminded of the difference in their ages.

Adriana turned to watch the rattletrap red pickup pull into the clearing beside her. He leaned out the open window, waving a newspaper, the boyish grin even more irresistible than before. She glanced at the newspaper on the seat beside her. Then she realized. He hadn't followed her at all, but simply come to answer the same ad.

"You're in the market for a brass bed, right?" His satisfaction at the coincidence was a little too obvious. He grinned as he opened her door and helped her out.

"I'm afraid so," she said, trying to sound aloof. "But I won't be any competition for you. I haven't found one yet that I can afford. Even the brass-plated ones with scrollwork are up around four hundred dollars."

"You don't want all that scrollwork, anyway," he said. "Brass demands clean, straight lines." She watched his eyes take on the same inquisitive brightness they'd had when he'd explained about butterflies. She listened with quiet admiration as he rambled on about brass beds, filling in details she hadn't read in any of her books. His kind of wisdom was common in the country people, she reminded herself. He had that unquenchable curiosity that was sometimes entirely lacking in someone who had completed four years of college.

"Are you goin' to stand out there and talk all evening or are you comin' in?" A tall, wiry farmer appeared in the doorway of his house and ushered them in. "Like as not I'll be milkin' till midnight," he muttered, then nodded politely to Adriana before replacing his weatherbeaten straw hat.

Adriana squeezed into the low-ceiling living room, then stopped in surprise. A wide-screen television supported by four huge stereo speakers stood against one wall. She counted at least four more stereo speakers, an elaborate music system, a videotape recorder and a small movie projector.

"Looks like we've won the New York State Lottery," the old man grumbled, "but it's just my son the high-powered New York attorney. He's sent us so much of this new-fangled electronic gadgetry that we've got no room for the old stuff. And half of it won't even work." He gestured toward the second set of speakers. "Couldn't get anything out of them big ones, so he just up and sent us these last week."

Adriana watched the copper-blond head bend with predictable interest over the elaborate electronic system. He flipped dials, fiddled with the switches at the back and immediately the room filled with bluegrass fiddle music. The old man slapped his knees in glee.

"You had the jacks switched," the younger man shouted over the music, "and this thing has an electronic safety switch that cuts off the speakers before they blow. You probably turned up the volume when you couldn't get sound."

The old farmer pumped the younger man's hand and then led them through the dining room, past an old woman cheerfully snapping string beans in front of a portable Sony color TV. In the small back bedroom a king-size bed, armoire and chest, all done in heavy Spanish style, dwarfed the antique brass bedframe propped against one wall. The rich luster of its polished metal seemed to radiate warmth. Adriana fingered the small test magnet she carried in her pocket. Knowing it wouldn't stick to the bedframe, she crossed the room, drew it out and tried, anyway. The magnet slipped to the floor. *Solid brass,* she thought excitedly as she stepped back to admire the clean, straight lines, the flattened ball finials and perfectly proportioned mushroom feet.

"Is it for yourselves?" the old man asked, "or do you own a shop?"

Adriana turned, looked from the expectant old man to the nonchalant younger one. "It's not for *us,*" she stammered. "That is, it's not for *both* of us." The top of the coppery-blond head bent, ignoring her predicament, and pretended to search for the fallen magnet. She caught just a corner of his suppressed grin. "We've only just met," she said, her voice gathering exasperation. "In fact, I don't even know his name."

"Out buying a bed already. Heh, heh." The old man laughed uproariously as Adriana felt her face grow hot, more with frustration than embarrassment.

"Haines Scott," he said, dropping the magnet into her open palm. "My friends call me 'Scotty.'" The small piece of metal felt warm, or was it the brush of his fingertips? "I'm looking for something a little different." He spoke to the farmer but his eyes continued to hold hers. She watched them brighten, saw the laugh lines deepen. "I'd like a little more decoration, maybe some scrollwork."

But you said... Her mind formed the words, but she did not speak them.

"It may be plain but it's a heck of a lot easier to polish than them fancy ones," the old man cajoled. "How about you, missy?"

"I'll give you three hundred dollars for it," she said, and held her breath. "Cash."

"Sold!" the old man bellowed. "Best offer I've had all day. Take it away."

"I can't," Adriana said as she took out an envelope and counted out all but one of the twenty-dollar bills. "I'll have to come back with my brother's truck."

"Can I help?" Haines Scott offered quickly. The same phrase, the same light, familiar country cadence, she thought, remembering his earlier roadside offer of help. How could she refuse?

"I'd be willing to pay you," Adriana offered, pulling the last twenty-dollar bill from the envelope.

"No," he said steadily, his brown eyes flickering over hers. "Just cook me dinner."

"I...don't cook," she stammered.

"Well that's okay, because I do," he said. "I've got a couple of stops to make first. How about eight?"

"Fine," she answered, "but I'm baby-sitting my niece and nephew."

"So I'll bring enough for four." She saw that he was determined. It was, she supposed, a date...sort of. She wondered vaguely if Calvin would mind, although they had long ago agreed that exclusivity would only come with engagement.

"My name is Adriana Anderson," she said.

They wrapped the bed in old blankets and loaded it into the back of the truck. The farmer insisted she take the box springs and mattress. "Law says I can't sell 'em," he said, "but I can give 'em away." Adriana thanked him warmly. He'd given her an especially good deal, and she knew they were all aware of it.

She watched the old man move off toward the weatherbeaten barn until his figure merged with the long shadows cast by the setting sun. In the distance she heard the slow, gentle lowing of the cows.

"Adriana." Haines Scott slid her name over his tongue, pronouncing each syllable with infinite care. She dared not turn to him and so continued watching the sun sink slowly behind the barn. "It means 'woman of the sea'—Latin, the feminine of Adrian." The lightness was back in his voice, the safe, familiar country friendliness.

"My father's name was Adrian," she said, rushing quickly past her painful memories. "Names, cooking, brass beds and butterflies—is there *anything* you don't know something about?"

"For starters, I haven't got the vaguest idea where you live," he said, the serious tone belying his broad grin.

"James Street." She scribbled the number on the back of her receipt. "You can't miss it. Rome, New York, is not that big unless you count the air force base, and of course, no one ever does."

"I'll find it," he called, watching her as he backed up the truck, then turned, narrowly missing the bed of yellow crysanthemums. "See you around eight."

Adriana stood for a moment watching the truck bounce from one rut to another. She was glad, as usual, that she'd ignored Calvin's advice. Small towns were just like that—you could trust people right off the bat. And she couldn't believe her luck—a solid brass bed for three hundred dollars. And free delivery, to boot.

As she headed down the road toward home, Adriana wondered what Haines Scott would cook for supper.

Chapter Two

The resonant chimes of the grandfather clock in the downstairs hall echoed through the sparsely furnished house in eight lonely peals. Adriana paused and stared at her reflection, her brush half through its last long stroke of her hair. She needed rugs. It would be a pity to cover the solid oak floors she'd labored over with sander, steel wool and epoxy-coated paintbrush, but until she could afford more furniture, she'd have to do something about those echoes. As she turned from the cheval floor mirror and crossed the otherwise empty room to her closet, her high heels clicked on the bare wood floor, aggravating the lonely quietness of the old house. Definitely. Rugs could be next on the list. Perhaps she ought to have waited for a bed.

Adriana selected a cream-colored, cowl-necked sweater and a cranberry jumper. Empire waisted, it hung loose and flowing. It's comfortable enough for managing the children, she told herself as she turned in front of the old-fashioned mirror. She watched the blush that always hovered in her lightly olive-colored skin deepen to a healthy rosiness and spread down her cheeks, pausing to tint the natural pinkness of her full, sensuous mouth. Maroon was her best color. She wondered if he'd notice. She caught herself at the thought and self-consciously turned away from the mirror. Rummaging in the top drawer of the built-in closet storage area, she finally found what she was looking for. Calvin's small gold signet ring slid easily onto her right-hand ring finger.

She heard the rattle of the loose bumper on the pickup as he stopped at the Linden Street light. The sound seemed to echo through the quiet neighborhood, all but empty for the Labor Day weekend. Adriana thought for a painful moment of other years, of family picnics. Warm reunions. She turned quickly, switched off the bedroom light and descended the stairs.

On the landing she paused to close the large casement windows and draw the filmy lace curtains.

At the sound of the truck door opening and closing, she hurried down the stairs, out the double front doors, onto the broad, softly lit front porch. In the chill of early evening she hugged herself and shivered, wondering one last time how she happened to have invited a complete stranger to dinner. *Haines Scott*. She repeated to herself the odd-sounding name. No wonder they call him Scotty.

Adriana leaned over the latticed railing of the front porch and watched as he unloaded two grocery bags from the back of the pickup. He swung up the front sidewalk in long, confident strides. The lamplight caught in his copper-gold hair, and she saw that it was brushed, though it still defied anything close to neatness. He was clean-shaven and smiling. Avoiding his eyes, she studied instead the rich, dark blue color of his wool sweater. The shade was a natural for him, she decided.

"Can I help?" she called out, moving down the front steps to meet him.

"That's my line," he said, reminding her of their first meeting. "You look great; that color becomes you." She could not avoid his eyes then, and found herself swimming helplessly in his gaze of unreserved intimacy, made acceptable somehow by its friendly tinge of humor. She tried to regain control by reaching for a bag of groceries. Her cool hand brushed against his warm one. He caught it, pressed it softly, let it go. Adriana felt her heart pause, skip beats and flutter on.

"Smells wonderful," she said, calming herself in the rich aroma that rose from the bag.

"I thought we'd go Italian," he said. "Kids always like spaghetti. Are they here yet?"

"Not yet," she answered. "My brother's dropping them off shortly."

"Good," he said. "I'll get the bed in and then you can show me this incredible house."

"Do you like it?" She felt pride flow in and fill her voice.

"It's the best one on the street," he said. "Even in this light I can see that you've kept the basic integrity. No unsightly modern additions. I like skylights, for example, but they look ridiculous atop a pitched Queen Anne-style gable."

He followed her through the small vestibule, down the front hall and into the kitchen. Setting his bag beside hers on the old porcelain-enameled drainboard, he stepped back to survey the room.

"Kitchens are a different story," he said, running an experienced hand across the lightly sanded surface of the overhead cabinets. She'd finished them just that morning, and as his palm swept across their smooth surface she had the odd feeling that he was caressing not the cabinets, but her face. "The kitchen is the heart of the house," he continued. "It's got to be kept modern."

"I've got a lot to do in here still," Adriana answered. "A new sink and lower cabinets are on order. My brother knows someone who's going to help me put them in. I'm afraid I don't have much imagination when it comes to kitchens, though. My mother was a marvelous cook and there never seemed to be much reason to learn."

"It's never too late," he teased. "It may come in handy someday when you have a family."

Adriana bristled. Why did people assume that having children was a given? Next he'd be asking why she wasn't married. Nervously she twisted Calvin's signet ring. "I don't plan to have a family," she said, ignoring the flash of interest that lit his cool gaze. "And it *is* too late. To learn from my mother, I mean. She and my father were killed six years ago. Their plane crashed on the way to an air force assignment in Turkey."

Adriana delivered the information quickly, the short clipped, businesslike sentences she'd adopted to hide the painful memories she'd only recently begun to face again. His eyes hovered over hers. She thought she saw the hungry look again, then something close to sympathetic recognition replaced it. For a moment she feared he'd press the subject further.

"I'm sorry" was all he said. Gratefully she turned to the groceries, unloading crisp lettuce, satiny red tomatoes, glossy green peppers.

"Can you make a salad?" he asked, eyeing her dubiously. She laughed and nodded. "Good," he said. "I'll get the bed. Where do you want it?"

"The large front bedroom," she answered. "Up the stairs and to the left. Do you think you can handle it alone?"

His look said, *You've got to be kidding, lady*. As he pulled off the heavy wool sweater she took a single, surreptitious glance and silently agreed. Beneath the snug-fitting, white jersey turtleneck, his muscles strained suggestively.

"I'll get the door," she said awkwardly.

"Don't worry about it," he said, expertly propping open the screen door with a small metal ring she'd never noticed before. "You just get busy on the salad. And put on a big pot of water for the spaghetti," he called from the porch, "with a teaspoon of salt."

Obediently she turned back to the kitchen, donned a white bibbed apron, put on the water and busied herself at the sink, shredding the lettuce. It seemed peculiar to be following someone else's orders in her own house. *Orders?* She pushed the vague suspicion to the back of her mind.

She counted his trips up the stairs, two for the frame, one for the box springs, one for the mattress. By the third trip he'd learned to negotiate the turn on the landing. She listened for the groan and masculine expletive but heard instead his hearty sigh of satisfaction. Adriana smiled to herself and began to dice the tomatoes into crimson cubes.

She was tossing the salad when she heard Tony's honk. She stirred the boiling spaghetti, dried her hands on her apron and hurried toward the door. Her brother waved from the street, shouting something about the red pickup that Adriana couldn't hear over the clamor of the children's voices.

Scrambling for their belongings, the two youngsters jumped out of their father's truck and raced each other up the sidewalk to where she waited on the porch. Licia's six-year-old legs were longer than her five-year-old brother's, but Tony, Jr., always traveled light and so he made it up the steps and into her arms well ahead of his overburdened older sister. She hugged the small boy around his roly-poly middle and bent to plant a quick kiss on Licia's upturned nose. The children vied for her attention as Adriana stood and waved to her brother. Licia's hand clutched hers tightly and Tony, Jr., clung to her skirt. Laughing, she gathered up their overnight things and turned toward the door.

He stood, motionless, framed against the etched glass oval of the door, toolbox in one hand, a wrench in the other. He'd put the bed together, she thought gratefully and started to thank him for his effort. But something in his stance and steady gaze made her hesitate, stand silently, as though posing for a photograph he was taking of the three of them with those faintly troubled, honey-colored eyes of his.

"Uncle Scotty!" The small girl shrieked in joy and left her side. He bent to drop the tools and gather the child in his arms. Even Tony, Jr., let go of her skirt and reached for the man she'd thought had been her exclusive discovery. A dark premonition clutched at Adriana's heart and squeezed it shut.

"I thought Tony might be your brother," he explained over the heads of the squealing children. "The last name could have been coincidental, but when you mentioned your parents, I figured the story was too similar—"

"You're my brother's friend," she interrupted coldly, "the air force test pilot who likes to cook." She saw him sense her withdrawal immediately and noted with satisfaction that his own gaze became cool and distant. Perhaps Tony had told him of her disdain for getting involved with transient air force personnel. "You're the one who's supposed to help me with the kitchen," she added.

"In exchange for Italian cooking lessons at Tony's Restaurant," he supplied carefully.

Slowly Adriana took off the apron and draped it over her shoulder. She should have known. The elaborate chronographic watch was a dead giveaway. The confident nonchalance, always in control, was another. Even the air force blue of his sweater was a natural. "Have you been at Griffiss Air Base long?" she asked, breaking the strained silence settling between them.

"About a year," he responded, then bent to swing a squealing Tony, Jr., to his shoulders. The tension between them eased in the children's laughter. He turned toward the kitchen.

"Then they'll be moving you again soon," she mused, following close behind him with Licia and the children's belongings. One by one she was removing memories of the afternoon and carefully filing them away.

When he stopped and turned suddenly, she almost collided with him. The spicy scent of his musky cologne filled her nostrils, trapping the very memory she'd just discarded. She watched the troubled look return to haunt his eyes. "They won't move me until I've finished my house," he said intensely, "and your kitchen."

Adriana backed away, startled by his vehemence. Immediately he regained control. "Besides, I'm working on a laser project for RADC and I can't believe they'll let me go until... that is, we're very close to finishing..." He turned, set Tony, Jr., on the counter and began to wash his hands, slowly, methodically. Adriana recognized the evasive attitude toward what was obviously a top-secret operation. Life in an air force family had long ago accustomed her to such behavior.

"My brother told me about your houses," she said casually, searching for an acceptable topic of conversation. Absently she twisted Calvin's ring, moved it without thinking to her left-hand ring finger. "He said you have several of them scattered across the country."

"A hobby," he said, turning toward her, drying his hands, eyeing her nervous gesture with the ring. "You're engaged?" he asked, nodding toward her hand.

She stared at what she'd done, embarrassed, moved the ring back to her right hand.

"Yes. Almost. No." The indecisive words tumbled out so quickly that she laughed with him at herself.

"Well, we're both in the same boat, then," he said, his easy familiarity returning. "I guess I'm married to the U.S. Air Force."

"In the same boat?" she asked.

"The same *unavailable* boat," he answered, swinging Tony, Jr., to the floor. "Guess that means we'll have to settle for friendship. That is, if you're willing." His eyes swept hers and lingered. She saw the subtle challenge in his eyes.

Friendship? Why not? Of course it couldn't grow much in the short time he was likely to be stationed in Rome. And he did realize that anything else was out of the question. What did it matter that he thought she was committed to Calvin? He had his own... commitment. Her mind ticked off his innumerable interests as he turned to the stove, grunted over the potentially overcooked spaghetti and reached for the colander.

"Friends, of course." Any friend of Tony's... she added mentally. She met his outstretched hand over the heads of the two small children and tried to suppress the sudden warmth that spread like wildfire through her body at his touch.

Adriana helped the children carry their overnight bags upstairs to the small bedroom over the kitchen. The homey clatter of pots and pans followed them up the stairway as Scotty rummaged in the cabinets looking for utensils. She helped the children make up their cots, lay out their nightclothes and wash for dinner. Tony, Jr., was already rubbing sleepy eyes as she gathered him in her arms and paused in the doorway of her own room.

Licia squealed and bounced immediately into the middle of the newly assembled bed. Adriana caught her breath but saw that he'd assembled the bed securely; it hardly moved under the child's weight. And the bed fitted the room perfectly. She'd be able to wake mornings to sunlight streaming in through the large bay window. Adriana sat down on the edge of the bed and shifted the weight of the sleepy child to her other shoulder. Licia scrambled over and stretched out her small arms in an affectionate hug.

Beyond, in the tilt of the cheval mirror, Adriana caught a picture of herself with the children. She smiled, giving in to a wistful savoring of the moment. She saw herself in the future, watching the children grow up, but she also saw, though she tried to repress it, a picture from the past. Herself, her brother, her mother, in other years, happier times. Adriana brushed away a single tear.

When she looked again, Haines Scott had filled out the picture. She stared. It was as though the four of them had been caught forever in one timeless moment. Again she imagined that he was photographing them. Storing the image for some distant lonely winter evening. She looked away. "I didn't hear you come up," she said over her shoulder.

"You were engrossed," he answered, taking Tony, Jr. "Do you like the bed?"

"It's perfect. Quite an improvement over my cot in the downstairs study. I'll have to get some full-size sheets," she added as an afterthought.

"Sheets?" She watched his eyebrows arch in surprise and read his question.

"I really don't have much, as you can see," she said. "There wasn't any sense in shipping all those household things back from Turkey. Mother and Dad had rented this house already and the tenants were settled. I was just starting at Utica College and Tony was engaged to Felicia and rooming with her parents."

"But weren't there things...personal things..." She watched the brown-gold eyes cloud with something she could not quite name.

"Not really," Adriana answered. "You know the air force. You move every two years. My mother saw it as a recurring opportunity to redecorate—out with the old and in with the new. Our house always looked like the latest edition of *Better Homes*. It was her way of coping, I guess."

"And yours is to stay put, to surround yourself with tradition."

Adriana smoothed her hair back from her temple impatiently. "Why not?" she retorted. "That brass bed is likely to be around long after I'm gone."

"And your 'almost' fiancé. Does he agree?"

He was prying and she felt defensive. "Calvin? Oh, he'll never leave the area. I lived with his mother while I was going to graduate school in Syracuse. She's been in central New York for generations. She'd never dream of moving. Cal's the same."

Later, over dinner, she watched him push the last of his spaghetti back and forth across his plate. His head was lowered, and she could not see his expression. It had been a wonderful meal, the first she'd ever remembered in her own home that seemed...complete, somehow. She supposed it was the children and their familiarity with both herself and Scotty that made her feel as though she'd known him much longer than a single afternoon and evening.

When he raised his eyes to hers over his plate, his look was pensive. Was it wistfulness that tinged his voice? "Sounds like you're all set," he said. "This house, a secure job, a new brass bed."

"You like antiques, too," she said, trying to fill the suddenly awkward space between them.

"I'm beginning to," he said, the gold flecks dancing again in his brown eyes. "My next move is likely to require a van. I've had enough of living out of a suitcase."

"I suppose you've moved a lot, too, being in the air force?" she asked with guarded sympathy.

"Not just since I've joined the air force," he said. The statement was short and unemotional. He stared straight at her, almost *through* her as he continued. "My father was an architectural contractor," he said. "His reputation extended worldwide. We...I frequently moved with him from site to site."

"That's where you get your talent for building," Adriana said.

"I suppose," he answered. "Now I'm going to put these two kids to bed. You make order here and then we'll have that tour. I want to see what you've done with this house."

She watched him hoist the kids up, one in each arm. It was funny that Tony had never introduced them. But then, she knew her brother was well aware of her prejudices. He knew how carefully she chose her friends. Most of them had lived in Rome their entire lives and their parents and grandparents before them. It was as though she didn't want, ever again, to get close to someone who might leave her.

Excited shouts and the bang of the bathroom door interrupted Adriana's thought. Then quiet settled through the house, broken only by the distant resonance of Scotty's voice. No echoes, she mused, as though the house was finally too full for them. He was reading the children a story, she knew. She longed to climb the stairs, curl up and listen, too. Quickly she busied herself, clearing the table, filling the sink with dishwater, pushing thoughts of Haines Scott into a far corner of her mind.

She was elbow deep in soapy water when he returned to the kitchen. "Cute kids," he said, brushing by her shoulder, destroying her resolve with the simple gesture.

"They liked your spaghetti," she said guardedly.

He laughed then, a slow easy sound that reminded her of water sliding over an open lock on the Barge Canal. "It's their father's sauce," he said. "Tony's raised those kids on it."

They settled into an easy silence. She washed, rinsed and handed him the dishes. He dried and set them in the cabinet overhead. He seemed to . . . to fit so *well*. Her mind stumbled over the thought, and she began to work more quickly.

"Where shall we start the tour?" she asked, taking the towel from him and hanging it up to dry.

He moved past her into the large dining room. She flipped off the light in the kitchen and quickly reached for the dining room wall switch. She flipped it once, twice, but the room remained bathed in the soft glow of the porch light as it shone in through the front window of the living room beyond. In the semidarkness, Adriana became acutely aware of the man beside her, the brush of his arm against hers, the lingering scent of his musky after-shave. Nervously she reached again for the wall switch. This time, light flooded the room at her touch.

"I don't know why that happens," Adriana said, breaking the silence. "I really need to have the wiring checked."

She saw immediately that he would appreciate all the things about the house that she herself loved best. He moved first toward the big bay window in the dining room. From its cushioned seat she often sat and looked out the tall, undraped casement windows at the squirrels and birds playing in the large lot between her house and her neighbor's. He ran a knowing hand up the carefully refinished oak of the woodwork, then traced the lead lattice of the stained glass strip at the top. She wished she could show him the window with sunlight pouring through it, creating kaleidoscopic colors on the polished floor below.

As he moved into the living room, she followed. He paused at the fireplace and stroked the smooth wood of the hand-rubbed oak mantelpiece. Adriana shivered. Again it was as though in stroking her house, he caressed her body. Nervously she rearranged the two cloisonné vases as she'd done at least a hundred times since Calvin had brought them to her a week ago.

"New?" he asked.

"Yes," she answered, "a birthday present." She moved the vases farther apart on the mantel. "Just put them to one side," he suggested. "Add something else to balance the other side. When's your birthday?"

"September twenty-third," she answered, "the equinox. I'll be twenty-six."

"Oho," he crowed. "No wonder we have so much in common. I'll be thirty-four on the same day!" He stood so close that she almost felt the warmth burn from his eyes into her own.

"So much in common?" She felt it, too, but wouldn't let on.

"Butterflies," he said. "Brass beds and Tony's kids, for starters."

"And friendship," she said, reminding him, and herself, of the limits they'd set.

"And friendship," he agreed, his arms slipping about her waist. The kiss was light, gentle, feathering her lips the way the butterfly had feathered her fingers. He tasted cool and tangy. She wasn't at all sure what sort of kiss it was. Before she could sort out her thoughts, he had released her and was moving across the living room.

"What's in there?" he asked, indicating a half-closed door off the front hall.

"It's just my study," she answered.

"Good grief! Look's like you're writing an encyclopedia." Several papers fluttered to the floor as he opened the door. Adriana bent to recover them.

"It's my thesis," she said. "I'm almost finished. It's a collection of original short stories." She made a hasty effort to straighten the papers.

"At least you won't be sleeping here...after you get the sheets," he said. She watched his eyes linger on the unmade cot and felt again as though he'd touched her in some intimate way. Hurriedly she turned aside.

Together they climbed the stairs and looked in on the sleeping children.

"Felicia," he whispered. "Latin name meaning 'happy,' and Anthony, also Latin, 'of inestimable worth.'"

The beauty of the description swept over Adriana and she stared wide-eyed at Haines Scott.

"I've always been curious about names," he said almost apologetically.

"And what does Haines Scott mean?" she asked dreamily.

He looked at her a long time before he spoke. As if clearing her for top-secret information, she thought whimsically.

"Haines is for Haines, Alaska," he said at last. "My father was building a house there when I was born. My mother hated the place. She must have been out of it when they brought in the birth certificate papers." He laughed again, but this time it did not remind Adriana of gently falling water. It was a cold laugh. Perhaps it was the thought of Alaska.

She showed him the small sewing room and the screened porch off it. He helped her lower the bamboo blinds and close a window that had been stuck open since she'd painted two weeks ago. Back in the hall, at the door to her bedroom, he hesitated. Adriana edged by him and opened the door opposite her own. "Want to see the attic?" she asked nervously.

In the dimly lit hallway, she tried to read his expression. It was as though he felt at home, as though he was the owner and she the visitor. "Lead the way," he said politely.

She climbed the steep staircase quickly, Scotty close on her heels. At the top, she stepped out onto the wide, unfinished floorboards and groped for the light chain. It flickered, then lit. The huge empty attic stretched before them like the long empty loft of an old abandoned barn.

"It's perfect for a dormitory...if you decide on a large family," he said thoughtfully.

"I told you," Adriana said, feeling the tension tighten her usually quiet voice and raise its tone an octave. "Calvin and I won't be having any children." She ignored his bemused stare and strode past him to the front area of the attic, intending to close the huge window that hung binlike into the large room. She struggled alone for a moment. "Scotty, will you please help me with this?" she asked finally. Overhead, the single naked light bulb flickered and dimmed.

He came to her then and together they pushed the window closed. As it slid into place, Adriana felt the man's body brush gently against her own. The moment seemed to stretch into timelessness. She felt her own body freeze as if awaiting some as yet unspoken order.

"Adriana," he said, his lips so close to her ear that his breath ruffled the hair at her temple. "Look. There. Beyond the corner of the house."

She stared, transfixed, in the direction he'd indicated. A few yellow leaves floated downward in the lamplight and she thought of the fallen butterflies they'd seen that afternoon. Then she saw it. The electrical box moved in the breeze and pulled away from the house as the bough of the tree rubbed against the wires.

"That may be your problem," he whispered. Was it possible? His voice sounded closer, more intimate almost husky.

Wiring, she thought. Of course. Before the rugs. Very first paycheck. And then she felt herself being turned in his arms, pulled closer into the warm, secure embrace. He tipped her head with a feather-light touch at her chin, then stroked her throat slowly, gently, to where it disappeared into the dip of her cowl-neck sweater. She felt his first kiss there, just above her heart, his warm breath trailing downward, sweeping the arc of her breasts with its caress. She felt him smooth her hair back from her temples with more kisses, and then, holding her head in both his hands, he covered her mouth with his own. Warm, hungry, searching, his kiss coaxed her own until she could not help kissing him back, tangling her hands in his hair, pulling him deeper into her mouth. She felt his arms tense about her, linger, relax and then draw back. He hugged her quickly, then stepped away.

She felt a sense of incredible loss mixed with tangled confusion as he moved toward the stairs. "I'd better be going," he said, his voice reverberating with the same unsteadiness she felt. Nonetheless, his tone was light, almost casual.

Before she could collect herself, Haines Scott was gone. Adriana lingered in the doorway, staring down the empty street, until she grew chill with the night air. Shivering, she twisted Calvin's ring until it grew warm against her cold hand.

Chapter Three

Adriana woke slowly, something lingering at the edge of her memory the way peeled oranges leave their pungent odor long after the fruit has been eaten. She turned in her small cot, the telltale crinkle of typing paper penetrating her consciousness. "Oh, no," she groaned. She sat up in bed, pulled up the quilt and tried to sort the mass of wrinkled papers that was her latest story. The whole thing would need to be retyped. Darn! Would she *ever* get the thesis finished?

It's my own fault, she reminded herself. I should never have moved back and taken on this house before I'd finished. She tucked her feet into comfortable slippers, pulled on her robe and reconsidered. The newly refinished louvered shutters glistened beautifully against the freshly painted cream-colored walls of the study. She tilted the bar and spikes of sunshine penetrated the small room, spreading across the stack of finished stories. The stories were good. She knew it.

And how could she be sure she could have written as well elsewhere? She stacked the rumpled papers and placed them on the desk. The children were up. She could hear them in the kitchen. The story could wait.

Adriana arrived just in time to see Licia overturn a bowl of soggy cornflakes into Tony's hair. The small boy sat for a moment, dolefully looking from his sister to his aunt, then broke into a loud wail. Licia stood in the center of the kitchen, her thin face screwed into a pout, large tears rolling down her face.

Adriana sighed. What happened to the angels we put to bed last night? she thought. *We?* The troubling thought she'd woken with planted itself squarely in her consciousness. Haines Scott. He certainly had a strange way of showing friendship.

"Mom says we're supposed to let you sleep," Licia said through sobs. "And Tony, Jr., wouldn't eat his cereal."

Adriana crunched across the kitchen, grinding cornflakes into the linoleum with every step. The sound made all of them laugh. How could she laugh and scold them at the same time? Her usual permissiveness winning out, she simply grabbed tissues for both the children and wiped away all traces of their tears.

Maybe Calvin was right. Neither of them knew the first thing about raising kids. And there was the question of their careers. And Calvin's age. Forty-five was just right for taking on the job of dean of Utica College, he'd reminded her, but a little late for starting a family.

"Come on you two, let's get this mess cleaned up and get your baths." She tossed Tony, Jr., a sponge, and he proceeded to move the spilled milk and soggy cereal from one side of the kitchen table to the other. Adriana grimaced as it slid through the crack where the table joined and dripped to the floor underneath. Meanwhile, Licia did her best to sweep up the cornflakes. Adriana tried not to watch. She busied herself at the stove, spreading butter, sugar and cinnamon on fresh slices of bread. What did it matter? she thought to herself. Her moments with the kids were too few, too precious to waste in scolding.

"Where's Uncle Scotty?" Tony, Jr., asked between bites of warm toast. Adriana groped for an appropriate answer as she watched the small pink tongue dart out to trap the bits of sugar clinging to his mouth and cheeks.

"He's gone home, silly," Licia answered for her. "He doesn't live here, you know."

Adriana felt her cheeks color at an embarrassment she could not define. Over the brim of her coffee mug, she eyed the empty chair. Scotty's chair. In one short evening he'd made it his own....

"Bath time," Adriana announced, interrupting her own, far too disturbing, thoughts. Tony, Jr., scrambled down off the stack of old Sears catalogs piled in his chair and headed up the stairs. Licia lingered, preferring to wait and take Adriana's hand. At the feel of the small fingers clasped about her own, Adriana felt warmth rise in her chest and spread upward. Impulsively she bent and hugged the child affectionately.

The old-fashioned clawfooted bathtub was a favorite with the children who could hardly wait for her to fill it and add the bubble bath she kept especially for them. Carefully she hoisted each child into the fragrant bath, then tossed them the small bag of toys she kept in the vanity. "We don't have long, kids," she said. "Your mom and dad will be waiting."

While the children bathed and played, Adriana pulled her stool up to the dressing table and took up her brush. The long, methodical, leisurely movements as she pulled the brush through her hair carried her back to the previous evening. What had she felt when he'd taken her face in his hands, kissed her like that? She stared into the mirror now cloudy with steam from the bath and tried to read her own hazy reflection.

"Thanks so much, Adriana," Felicia Anderson said. Adriana felt herself delight in the warm embrace of her brother's wife. The small, full-figured woman turned and kissed her portly husband, then hurried the two dark-headed children into the family station wagon. Adriana waved, then turned to her brother.

"Aren't you going?" she asked. She thought fleetingly of all the Sundays that the entire Anderson family had filled up the third front pew of St. Peter's church. Maybe now that her thesis and the house were both nearly finished, she'd switch from Friday evening service and attend on Sunday mornings with Tony's family.

"I went to early church," her brother answered. "I've got to be around to supervise. Come on over to the restaurant and see what we've done so far."

Adriana hesitated, thinking of the work waiting for her at home. Then she looked into her brother's happy, settled face. There was no sense in arguing, she knew, when Tony wanted to talk restaurant. And she had a few questions of her own for him.

He closed the door of the modest white frame house that had belonged to Felicia's parents and their parents before them. Stuffed with antique furniture and treasured possessions, she marveled as always that he never bothered to lock the door. No one ever locked doors in this fertile river valley where Italian greengrocers had raised and sold their produce for generations.

She followed her brother as he picked his way down the path in the garden that lay between the house and restaurant. Adriana tried to keep to the dry areas of the path. The loose rich black dirt, known affectionately as "the muck," had a way of working itself into the crevices of all her shoes. *The muck*. She remembered as though it were yesterday, the rich smell of the newly turned earth, warm and fertile, the sound of soft cadences as her mother spoke Italian, asking the greengrocer when the first *pomodoro* would ripen.

As Adriana stepped aside to avoid a puddle, her leg brushed the branch of a tomato plant. One of the late-maturing fruit dropped to the soft earth at her feet.

"Keep it," Tony said when she offered him the pear-shaped crimson jewel. "Felicia's put up nearly enough to get the restaurant through the winter." He turned and continued down the path. "I'm convinced these tomatoes are going to make our sauce famous," he added over his shoulder. Adriana smiled at the enthusiasm that carried his voice back to her. She watched her brother's broad back move along before her and wrapped it in a mental hug. At times like these she knew she'd been right to stand by Tony and his dream.

"Felicia and I made ourselves stay away all day yesterday," Tony continued. "We took the kids and toured the Erie Canal Village, picnicked and so on.

Then last night was wonderful, just the two of us, candlelight dinner at home for a change. Thanks, Adriana." He took her hand to help her across the last of the puddles and squeezed her fingers affectionately before releasing them. "By the way, I noticed you had extra company for dinner, too."

She searched the warm blue eyes her brother turned toward her and blushed when she saw the tease rise up in them. "The famous bachelor fly-boy," he said. "The women in Rome are waiting in line to ask him to dinner. He gives them all at least one chance." He chuckled, but his look held something of a warning. Tony needn't worry, she thought. She certainly wasn't going to be part of some transient air force harem.

"Dinner was supposed to be compensation for his delivery of my bed," Adriana said carefully.

"Your bed!" Tony chortled. "How long have you known this guy?" She shoved him good-naturedly, then told her brother the story of how she'd met Haines Scott.

"He's a special guy," Tony insisted. "He knows what I mean when I talk about creative cooking. And if anyone can get me up in a plane, Scotty can."

Up in a plane? She searched Tony's face for the telltale shadow, the one reflection of the only thing that darkened his life. . . his persistent fear of flying. As she watched, beads of perspiration formed just below the hairline on her brother's furrowed brow. He reached for his handkerchief.

"Have you told Felicia yet?" she asked calmly.

Tony wiped his brow and absently folded and refolded the handkerchief. "No," he said and smiled wanly at his sister. "She thinks Scotty's doing your kitchen in exchange for the cooking lessons. I want her to be surprised...or at least not disappointed if I fail. You know she hasn't seen her mom and dad for two years. Since her dad's stroke they can't make the trip north every year."

"And you can't leave the restaurant long enough to drive to Florida."

"It's at least a three-day trip," Tony said. "But if we could fly, it would solve everything." Adriana watched the light return to his eyes, watched him reach, stretch himself toward bravado.

"You'll make it, Tony—I know you will." She said the words quietly, with all the confidence she could muster. And she'd say them over and over to him, as she'd done in past years. No matter how long it took, she'd keep trying to convince her brother that he was not living on borrowed time, that he had not been destined to die in the crash that took their parents' lives, that he had not been accidentally left off the fatal plane bound for Turkey. She'd keep reminding him, as the counselors at Hutchings Psychiatric Center had reminded him, that he had *chosen*, with her support and ultimately with their parents' support, to stay behind and follow his own path.

Tony pushed open the outer door of the restaurant, then held the inner one open for her. "You won't know the place," he said with obvious pride. "I wanted to keep the old tables and chairs," he said, indicating the country kitchen furniture of the front dining room, "so Felicia and I refinished the tabletops ourselves, and I had Louis clean and polish every rung of every chair."

"They look beautiful," Adriana said. "When did the new cushions come in?"

"Just last week," Tony answered as Adriana touched the plush red velvet. "Once they finish laying the new carpet, we'll be ready to open."

Leona, Tony's head waitress, called him over to help drape the new curtains Felicia had made for the big front windows. Then Adriana settled into a cushioned chair and relaxed. She had to admit the place was looking marvelous. They had removed the venetian blinds and polished the window glass until it shone in the sunlight. Plants hung invitingly overhead, and here and there were sparkling Tiffany lamps.

Adriana smiled in surprise as she picked out various pieces of antique furniture from Felicia's overstocked attic. The old rolltop desk made an excellent hostess area and the apothecary chests were a natural for the waitresses' stations. The restaurant belonged to Tony and Felicia completely now, in style as well as title.

She'd been a bit afraid for him at first, when he'd taken his share of the inheritance and bought out Felicia's parents. The old couple had wanted to retire to Florida, but the restaurant had made them anything but rich. And Felicia's two sisters had married factory men, hardworking but of modest means. But Tony had always loved cooking, even before he'd started working at the restaurant. He was a natural to take it over. And her worries had all been unfounded. The initial burst of competition from the new highway hotels had hardly fazed their business. She knew, without a doubt, that her brother had been born to be in this place, just as she felt totally, completely at home in their parents' house on North James Street.

"Tony!" Adriana jumped as the deeply masculine voice boomed through the entire restaurant. She followed her brother as he hurried through the back dining room and into the kitchen.

"You've got to keep these guys out of my kitchen," the burly man shouted. "They turned on the water in the *zuppa* and ruined the whole pot!"

"Angelo," Tony cajoled, "you can make more soup and it's bound to be better. They'll be finished in here in no time, and then you'll have a new kitchen as elegant as the dining rooms." The man raised pudgy arms skyward and returned with resignation to his work of preparing the crew's lunch. Adriana left Tony to console his new cook and went out to explore the back dining room.

Heavy damask drapes hung floor to ceiling, darkening the room with an intimate warmth. The round tables, covered with floor-length wine-colored cloths, held small hurricane lamps. Against the far wall, near the corner fireplace, Tony had hung several curio cabinets. Leona was dusting and positioning Felicia's collection of paperweights.

"They're exquisite," Adriana said as the waitress finished and closed the cabinet.

"This place will never be the same," she sighed. "Your brother and sister-in-law are in-de-fat-igable."

Adriana smiled at the waitress's precise diction. "Are you still taking night classes on the base, Leona?" she asked.

"Yes, and I hear you're teaching a class there this semester."

"Right," Adriana answered. She felt her chest tighten, her breathing tug against constricting muscles. It would be her first trip through the Skyline Gate of Griffiss Air Force Base since the memorial service for her parents had been held at the chapel six years ago. She'd politely refused later invitations from her parents' old friends, until one by one they'd all been transferred away. Now university classes were taking her back on base, just as they'd kept her from going to Turkey six years ago. Adriana forced her thoughts away from her nervousness and onto the preparation she knew she should be working on at home.

"Before you go," Tony said as he walked her outside, "I have something I want you to read." He pulled a crumpled letter from his pocket and pressed it into her hand. "It's from Aunt Beatrice," he said, his voice sounding small and far away.

Adriana removed the slip of blue notepaper from its matching envelope and fingered its feathered edge. She knew Tony was thinking of their mother, whose only grief had been the long estrangement from her sister. Until, of course, she and Tony had stood together against the move to Turkey.

Their mother had wanted Tony to finish his senior year at the American school in Ankara. He'd argued that he loved restaurant life, didn't want to go to college, didn't want to leave Felicia. And then he'd reminded their mother that she had been the one who'd taught him to cook in the first place. He'd learned to make his Italian mother's pasta even before he'd learned to play baseball. Adriana could hear him shouting the words as if it were yesterday. She also heard her own voice insisting she'd come home weekends from college to check up on him. *She understood you, Tony,* Adriana wanted to insist as she searched his troubled face.

"She wants us all to come to Washington for Thanksgiving, Adriana," he said, stumbling over the words. "You, me, Felicia and the kids. She says she'll pay the airfare..." His voice trailed off into a nervous laugh. Adriana sifted through her memory for the face of the small prim woman in the cameo portrait that had always set atop her mother's dresser. It had been so unlike their mother to keep mementos. "What's done is done," she would always say, but still the portrait of her sister had never been discarded. Tony had said it, too, when Aunt Beatrice had visited shortly after their parents' deaths. She'd been away at college when he'd called to tell her about it, to tell her how Aunt Beatrice had tried to explain her long silence, explain the quarrel that had caused a rift between the two sisters. "What's done is done," she heard Tony say in the darkness of her memory.

"The old man died at last—sclerosis of the liver of course," Tony said. "She's going to move to Florida next spring...wants us to take some of her furniture... Mother's things... Felicia and I have no use for more antiques," he hurried on. "And I can't spare the time from the restaurant. You could tell her we'll visit her in Florida... when we go to see Felicia's parents."

"Of course I'll go," she promised. "Heaven knows *I* can use some furniture."

She allowed her brother to crush her against him in one of his great bear hugs and luxuriated in the feeling. Their family had always been a touching one, and she missed that. Overt affection was not one of Calvin's distinctive characteristics.

"Don't forget tomorrow night," Tony called after her as she turned toward the garden path. "Dinner at

Ferantes' Ristorante." She knew he'd never drop Felicia's parents' name from the title of the restaurant. Things stayed the same here. She paused, bent and pulled off two of the bright red tomatoes. Already the vines had begun to wither and die. But she knew that there would be tomatoes here next year and the year after next. That made a difference.

Lost in thought, Adriana missed the turn. She passed her house, caught herself a block beyond and turned up the alley toward her garage. She parked, then lingered in the backyard to pick an armful of chrysanthemums from the bed beside the garage.

"Thought I'd stop and have another look at the kitchen," Haines Scott said as she came around the corner of the house. "I was about to give up on you."

She started. She'd missed the jeans-clad figure lounging in the porch swing. "I took the children home," she said. "Really, you needn't start right away."

"Good," he said and pulled her down on the porch swing beside him. "I always wanted to sit in one of these swings on a porch like this on a Sunday afternoon with a . . . friend."

"And then?" she asked coolly.

He nestled her close to him in response, pulled her head down on his shoulder and began to hum. She'd have to drop the chrysanthemums to push him away.

"All we need is moonlight," he answered.

"Then it wouldn't be Sunday afternoon," she retorted.

"Right," he said. "So we'd better get going."

"Going?" she said as he pulled her down the walk and tucked her into the passenger side of an ancient

Austin Healey Sprite. "Where's the truck?" she asked. He slammed the door, mashing the chrysanthemums.

"I only drive the truck when I'm hauling things!" he shouted over the roar of the noisy engine. "And we're going to my house. I want you to see my kitchen."

"Kitchen?" she mumbled. "Are you sure you don't mean your etchings?"

"Friends don't behave like that," he said. "You can trust me!" She watched the broad grin light up his face.

She wasn't at all prepared for his house. The twenty-minute drive had carried them quickly out of the city limits, past farmlands filled with dried cornstalks and fading pastures to a gently rising hill at the foot of Lake Delta. She'd expected something more traditional. Instead, the ultramodern house seemed all glass and wooden decks. Still, it looked natural against the woodsy setting, the lake stretched invitingly below it.

"I lived in California last," he explained from the window-walled living room overlooking the lake. "I'm always a step behind in my houses. Next time I move I'll probably build a two-story Victorian, regardless of the locale. My dad would turn over in his grave," he added, "believing as he did that a house should match its environment."

"Your father isn't living?" she asked.

"He fell off a roof he was inspecting on a house in Colorado Springs," he said. "Slid right off and broke his neck. I was sixteen." Adriana shuddered at his cool attitude, wondering if in time she'd feel the same distance about her own parents' death.

"And your mother?" she asked.

"Still in Colorado Springs," he answered bluntly. Adriana thought she detected a measure of tense constraint in the cool voice. "Come on," he said. "I'll show you the house."

Each of the two large upstairs bedrooms and adjoining baths looked out over a pleasant view of the hillside. He'd used no drapes, only miniblinds where privacy was needed. Sunlight seemed to wash the entire house. Adriana felt light and airy. She laughed when she saw the mattress in the middle of the floor, blankets flung aside, pillows askew. "You needed that bed worse than I did," she said. "At least I had a cot."

"What are friends for?" he asked. She caught a glimpse of...what was it? Wistfulness? No, something more akin to restless hunger. She looked from his eyes to the unmade bed and backed away. Her stomach felt like a butterfly had settled just below her navel.

"The kitchen," she said. "You were going to show me the kitchen."

She stood amid white Formica counters and pine cabinets, watching Scotty produce blender, bourbon and glasses from carefully organized hidden cupboards. From a clever turntable built into the corner of the cabinets, he pulled out a box of saltines. A wooden cutting board slid magically out from under the counter. He passed her a knife and a wedge of sharp New York cheddar.

"The idea," he explained as she sliced the cheese, "is to keep everything handy but completely out of sight. Whisky sour," he said, passing her the drink. "It's mostly lemonade."

They carried the platter of cheese and crackers and their drinks to the conversation pit in the living room.

Adriana settled into the soft beige velvet sectional and tucked her feet up under her while Scotty searched through his tape collection. In a moment, lively piano ragtime filled the vaulted room.

"The acoustics are fantastic," Adriana said. "And I like the sunlight. It seems to come from everywhere. It's a modern house, but warm somehow, and homey."

"I hope the buyers agree," he said quietly.

"You're selling it?" she asked. "Why, the deck isn't even finished."

"I'll have to sell one sooner or later," he said. "I can't just keep on building houses, moving away and renting to friends."

"How many houses do you have?" she asked.

"Finished or unfinished?" He placed one arm around her shoulders and stretched the other one across her as he reached for a slice of cheese. The pressure of his arm against her breasts made Adriana feel short of breath. She stared up into the cinnamon-colored eyes laced with lively yellow flecks.

"You don't have to, you know," she said, trying to still her racing heart long enough to make casual conversation.

"'Have to' what?" His breath was warm on her cheek.

"You don't have to move away and leave this house. Why couldn't you just leave the air force? Build houses for a living?"

"There's a contractor here who's after me to do just that," he answered. "But I tried it once. After Nam I went back to the Springs, supposedly for good. It didn't work. Flying's in my blood."

His words clinked together like the ice in his empty glass, turning her heart cold. Why should she care? She had her own plans. She knew he was looking her direction, his eyes burning into her mind, searching it. She looked away.

"Let's have a look at these books," he said. "We can make some decisions on your kitchen. You can . . . tell me what you like."

She blushed at the double entendre, then covered it with a protest. "I can't let you work on my kitchen. You've got enough to do here. Besides, I don't know if I can afford to do it that quickly."

"Didn't Tony tell you? The materials are his birthday present to you. My work is in exchange for his teaching me Italian cooking."

"I thought flying lessons were the trade," she said quietly.

She watched as Scotty's face registered surprise. "He told you?" he asked.

"Of course," she answered. "He tells me everything."

"Everything?"

"Everything. Now if we can just get down to business . . ." She opened the first catalog and thumbed through its contents. He brought out a sketchpad and ruler and drew a diagram of the kitchen. Occasionally their forearms brushed. The scent of his aftershave seemed to hang in the air between them. Adriana tried to take short, quick breaths, as though inhaling the scent of him too deeply would draw him further into her life.

"Have you considered countertop material?" he asked. "Terrazzo tile is interesting. You could face the wall around the table with it, too. The feel is nice..." His gaze was lingering somewhere above her lower lip.

Adriana shivered, then forced her attention to the breakfast nook. She laughed. "Tile might come in handy," she said, remembering Tony, Jr., the cereal bowl upturned on his head. She told him of the episode.

"I can't believe you don't want kids," he said. "You're a natural with those two."

She sidestepped the comment. "And you?" she asked. "Do you ever look toward marriage and a family?" She watched the gold flecks fade from his eyes, watched them harden and grow dull.

"I think *about* it," he said carefully. "But I don't look *toward* it. Family life and flying do not mix. For example, I've got to get to work."

"Work?" she asked incredulously. "It's Sunday afternoon of the Labor Day weekend!"

"SAC doesn't take holidays, sweetie, and one of their pilots is running my...experiment tonight."

"Of course," she said coolly. How could she have forgotten the countless weekends her own father had been called away by the U.S. Air Force.

He seemed high-strung on the trip back to town. Once he looked in her direction, then made some vague comment about the weather. She felt the distance expand and then contract between them like elastic thread.

"Try to find time to look through these," he suggested as he piled her arms with catalogs and magazines. "I'll be over to measure when I can."

She stood on the porch, waiting. She had no idea for what. "By the way," he said. "I brought you a present." He reached for a shopping bag he'd left under the porch swing, pulled out two sets of plastic-wrapped sheets and cases and tossed them on top of the magazines. "They're not monarchs," he said, indicating the butterfly pattern on the sheets, "but they reminded me of... you. BX was open late last night."

"Do you always go to the BX in the middle of the night?" she asked.

"It beats a cold shower in chilly weather," he answered. He turned as if to go, then turned back to her. His gaze was direct, open, demanding. And his mouth was just as firm. When she tried to pull away, his grip on her shoulder tightened, slid down her arms, his fingertips caressing the sides of her breasts. She thought for a moment of dropping the books on his feet. But his mouth clung to hers. Pliant, incessant, demanding... what? She fought the answer that her body began to give him—the sensitizing of her flesh, the floating feeling in her stomach, the way her breath grew short. When he paused for breath, Adriana whispered, "My brother told me all about you, Haines Scott, and I know your type—conceited, careless, perpetually single..."

She watched as the gold flecks in his eyes turned to glinting knives. The grin spread across his face almost as if he was using it to cover whatever else he felt. "You've got part of it right, anyway," he said. "Perpetually single. See you."

She sputtered, searching for words to tell him he could forget that. She didn't care if she never saw him again. But before she could answer, he'd sped away in the small red car, leaving her alone on the porch.

Chapter Four

All set for your first day of classes, Adriana?" Calvin's question was loaded and she knew it. As she swung the door wide, the knob hit the plaster wall hard enough to rattle all the hallway pictures. She'd about had it with men this weekend. Calvin had better not push his luck.

"I'm as ready as I'll ever be," she said as she took his coat and turned away before he could plant the customary kiss on her left cheek. She hung his coat in the hall closet, then turned back toward the kitchen.

Calvin failed to follow, and Adriana heard him rummaging in her study. Perhaps she should have tried to be a little warmer, she thought with misgivings. Nervously she tugged at the silverware drawer. Why did it always stick when she was in a hurry? Suddenly the drawer gave way completely. It flew toward her, scattering silverware, wooden spoons and an assortment of kitchen gadgets across the linoleum floor.

She was trying to untangle the tongs from the egg slicer when Calvin sauntered into the kitchen. He tossed the pile of rumpled paper that was her latest story on the table. From the middle of the strewn utensils, she looked up into his stern expression. For a moment, Adriana felt like a child about to be scolded by a none too loving parent.

"What happened to this?" he asked accusingly.

"I slept on it."

"Looks like it. Want me to edit?"

"No, Calvin. If I don't get this cake iced we're going to be late for Tony's party."

"So I'll just sit here and read while you work." She watched him settle his large frame into a kitchen chair. *Scotty's chair.* She pushed the thought away. Why couldn't Calvin just sit in the living room, as he usually did, and sort through her stack of the *Daily Sentinel*?

"Calvin, you know it makes me nervous when I have to watch you read my stories. I can't stand all those little noises you make. I always wonder what you're thinking. Put the story away, okay? You can sit here and talk to me. I've got some interesting news." She wanted to tell him about Haines Scott now. Telling would make it all right. He'd know she had simply met her brother's friend by accident and that was all there was to it. Wasn't it?

Calvin looked up from the manuscript. "I tried to get you all day yesterday, Adriana. I thought you were going to spend the weekend doing lesson plans."

She drew the knife across the top of the cake, trying to even up the swirls of icing. "Cal, you know I taught all through grad school. I could teach freshman English with my eyes closed."

"How about the beginning literature?" he asked. "And the fantasy literature course you're teaching at the air base night school?"

"I'm *ready* Calvin. Besides, I need to meet the students before I can plan further. Their interests have lots to do with how the class will move."

"Nonsense!" Calvin's favorite word grated on Adriana's nerves. He leaned over her shoulder, stuck a pudgy finger in the icing and licked it clean. Instinctively she moved aside. She felt his quizzical look follow her. "Where were you yesterday?" he asked outright.

Adriana took a deep breath and answered, the words tripping out quickly, in contrast to her usual measured cadence. "I was working on the kitchen."

"The kitchen? The phone is right there on the wall. Couldn't you stop long enough to pick it up?" His chin trembled slightly. She hated that. She never knew whether it meant he was feeling melancholy or about to get angry. She opted for the former and tried to sound sympathetic.

"I wasn't *here*, Calvin, I was...out. Meeting with Haines Scott, the man who's going to do the kitchen." There. That sounded very...ordinary, she thought.

"You're *having* it done?" Calvin lit a cigarette. Dutifully, she offered him an ashtray and moved to raise the kitchen window. Warmed by the late afternoon sun, the air drifted in, soothing her frayed nerves. She allowed her eyes to rest on the view of the garden in her neighbor's backyard.

"I'm not exactly having it done," she said slowly. "I've sanded the upper cabinets and walls myself, and the sink and lower cabinets are all on order. It was

Tony's idea. Scotty is a friend of his. And Tony's paying for the materials for my birthday."

Calvin took a long draw on his cigarette and blew the smoke toward the ceiling. "Well, at least Tony's got one practical use for his money," he said.

Adriana bristled at his comment, considered retorting and thought better of it. She was in no mood to argue with Calvin about how Tony was never going to make it if he didn't go to college and get at least an M.B.A.

"So is this friend of Tony's doing the work for nothing, or what?" Calvin's tone was guarded. Her hand trembling slightly, Adriana smoothed the last of the icing, returned the pan to the sink and turned on the water before answering.

"Well?" he prodded. She hated his prompting. He never gave her the time she needed for a thoughtful answer. On days like this she wondered if Calvin's annoying little idiosyncrasies would ever seem surmountable. Maybe after years of marriage... She watched the pan fill with warm water and stirred the murky mixture with the wooden spoon. "He's doing the kitchen in exchange for cooking lessons with Tony," she answered at last.

Calvin nearly choked on his cigarette smoke. "*Cooking lessons?* You've got to be kidding. What have we got here, another budding restauranteur?" He loosened his tie. It was new, she noticed, and he was overdressed, as usual; she'd have to change.

"Calvin, I'll just be a minute. Will you close the windows and turn off all the lights?"

Why did it always have to be like this? she thought as she quickly slipped out of her skirt and sweater. It seemed as though they sparred constantly. Yet they had so much in common...didn't they? She really should have let him read her story. His comments were always to the point. He was head of the history department and author of several texts on classical Greece, and his writing was impeccable.

She chose a wine-colored knit dress trimmed in velvet ribbons at the wrist-length sleeves and low square neck. As she turned in front of the cheval mirror she thought of the sumac trees turning crimson along the country road. Behind her, the butterfly print of the new sheets splashed across the unmade bed.

Adriana switched off the bedroom light and hurried to the living room. Calvin hated to be kept waiting. She noticed that he'd moved the cloisonné vases back to the center of the mantel. The rigidly balanced effect annoyed her. "They're Ming, you know," he said defensively. "Quite valuable."

"How much are they worth, Calvin?" she asked because she knew he'd insist on telling her. He named the price and Adriana drew in a sharp breath. With that amount of money she could have had the kitchen done twice over.

She watched him bask in her astonishment. "You know, Adriana, you really should get some sort of burglary protection. You've got the clock now and these vases."

And a beautiful new brass bed, she added to herself.

"I hear they have some terrific electronic systems. Or you could get a watchdog and chain him to the tree out front."

"What good would that do?" Adriana teased. "They'd just come in the back door. Besides, you're allergic to dogs."

"You know what I mean," Calvin responded impatiently.

Adriana smoothed her hair back from one temple. "Calvin," she said quietly, "you know that's one of the main reasons I live in Rome. I feel safe here. I don't *need* an electronic burglar alarm or a watchdog."

He strode toward her then and caught her roughly around the waist. "Live with me and you'll always feel safe, Adriana," he whispered in her ear.

"I . . . I'm not ready for that, Calvin," she said, her hands splayed against his heavy chest.

He continued to press her to himself. The bite of his large belt buckle in her upper abdomen was almost painful. "Adriana," he crooned in her ear, "it's been all summer. Let's forget the dinner at your brother's and spend the evening here alone."

She slipped out of his arms and backed tentatively toward the kitchen. "If we did that, what would I do with this cake? I'd have to eat it all by myself. You know you hate it when I put on weight." She laughed nervously.

Calvin shrugged, pulled out another cigarette and lit it with the gold lighter she'd given him five Christmases ago. It can't have been that long ago, she thought, a bubble of panic rising in her chest. But what would she have done without him then? She'd felt so terribly alone that first summer after college. New friends and new experiences had not assuaged the longing she felt for someone to write home to, someone to fill the huge void left in her life by the death of her parents. Tony had had Felicia, and she'd had . . . a summer job working on Calvin's research project. What would she have done without it, and him? She crossed the room, smoothed his tie, straightened his collar. "I like your new tie," she said, groping for sincerity.

"My mother's been asking about you Adriana," he said on the drive over. "She's wondering why we haven't been to Syracuse in a while."

"You can tell her it's my thesis... and your trip to Greece this summer," she said. "After all, it is the truth."

"She never could understand why you left her house in Syracuse every weekend all winter to come back to Rome to write." Calvin repeated the familiar theme. "You could have stayed in Syracuse on weekends. Then I'd have seen more of you. You might be ready to... to... I've hardly seen you all year, Adriana."

Why couldn't he say it? she thought. He was probably no more ready for commitment than she was. She knew without looking that his chin was trembling again. She reached out to touch his arm and tried, as she had so many times, to explain.

"I needed the quiet, Calvin," she said. "Working on the house made the ideas flow. I could finish sanding a wall and a whole story would be outlined in my mind. I'm sorry if your mother misunderstood. I'll always be grateful that she put me up while I was in graduate school."

They drove across the railroad tracks and pulled into the freshly graded parking lot. The new colonial-style sign hung discreetly from the gateposts at the corner. "Ferantes' Ristorante," Adriana read aloud with pride. "The 'Ristorante' was Tony's idea, a reflection of the quiet elegance he hopes to introduce in the back dining room."

"Quiet elegance?" Calvin's tone was condescending as he pulled his blue Mercedes in behind the scattering of older, less expensive cars.

"Calvin," she said and kissed him lightly on the cheek. "Please try to be nice."

"Aren't I always?" he said, feigning hurt. She watched him straighten his tie in the rearview mirror and knew he'd probably hold his own, despite her request.

"Tell them about your trip to Greece," she suggested as he helped her out of the car.

"Do you think they could follow it?" he asked.

"Really, Calvin," she snapped, "they are Italian you know."

"Except for you and Tony," he reminded her. "You're only half Italian and you hardly look it." Adriana chafed at the remark. Why couldn't he just accept her family for what they were? She'd done it for him, and his mother was not an easy person to please.

"You didn't tell me there would be kids," Calvin muttered under his breath as they pushed through the spotlessly clean outer glass doors into the bright front dining room of the restaurant. The children surrounded them, each demanding a hug from their favorite aunt. Licia and Tony, Jr., were joined by Felicia's sister's children. The bright array of fresh young faces made Adriana anxious for the start of classes, even though tomorrow's eager faces would be a little older. Licia took the cake from Adriana and bustled, as only prim little girls can, off toward the kitchen.

"She'll drop it," Calvin warned.

"No, she won't," Adriana reassured him. She steered Calvin out of the tangle of children, toward the small cocktail lounge that separated the front family dining room from the more elegant back one. Louis, her brother's best friend and bartender, waved a cheerful hello.

"You've got to see the glasses, Adriana," he called. "Tony got them in New York City." She watched Louis pull the top off the crate of glasses, remove one and hold it to the light. Rainbow prisms reflected off the thin glass into the mirror behind the bar.

"Ridiculous," Calvin snorted. "They're nice but for a *restaurant*? They'll all be broken within a week."

"Not if we are careful," Louis answered curtly. "Would you like a drink, Mr. Caufield?"

"Make it a Scotch on the rocks, Louis, and would you bring it to the table please." The small man's dark eyes flashed at Calvin's condescending tone, then softened and settled on his best friend's sister.

"I'll have a whiskey sour, please, Louis," she answered. "Light on the whiskey. And be sure to use one of the lovely new glasses."

"Yes, ma'am," he replied proudly. Adriana wanted to linger and ask Louis about his new baby daughter. Besides, they could carry their own drinks to the table. Louis obviously had a lot to do, and it *was* a family party.

But Calvin pulled her ahead. "We might as well get this over with," he hissed in her ear. She shot him an angry glance. Couldn't he just relax and enjoy himself? They *were* her family. All she had left, anyway. And someday they'd be his family, too. She tried to imagine it as they moved into the back dining room. The boisterous family table quieted suddenly as they approached.

"By the way," Calvin whispered, "when did you start drinking whiskey sours?"

"Adriana." Tony's warm greeting saved her from an awkward answer. "Hello, Calvin. I believe you know everyone." Adriana hugged her brother, then Felicia and Felicia's two older sisters. She nodded and shook hands with their husbands, two quiet, dark-haired men who, like Tony, loved their wives and children dearly.

"Frankie just got a promotion at Revere." Felicia nodded toward her sister's husband. "We were just about to propose a toast."

"Frank, that's great!" Adriana exclaimed.

"It's not a lot more money, but it is a step up," the young man explained shyly.

"Where *is* that boy with our drinks?" Calvin muttered under his breath.

Adriana felt her face flush at Calvin's impatience. "Guess I've had enough experience to get them," she said a little too brightly, knowing Calvin hated to be reminded of her cocktail waitressing days. But the job had gotten her through her first four years of college. Calvin was fond of reminding her that she could have gone in style if she hadn't insisted on using her inheritance to pay off the house.

"I'll get the drinks," Calvin said halfheartedly. She threw him a withering glance and strode off.

"Why do you put up with him, Adriana?" Tony asked, taking the tray from her. She flashed her brother a warning look. "Okay, okay," he said. "I'm sorry."

Adriana shrugged off the comment and returned to the table. Calvin finished his drink quickly and went off to the bar for another. As he relaxed, Adriana allowed herself to relax, also, enjoying the light conversation mingled with the distant laughter of the children in the adjoining room.

Now and then the youngsters came to whisper to their parents. Adriana laughed in pleasure when, for no apparent reason, Tony, Jr., came running to the table, pushed between herself and Calvin to climb into her lap and hug her hard. But with chagrin she saw Calvin mopping at his new tie where his drink had spilled on it. Quickly she put Tony, Jr., down and rose, her own drink in her hand.

"I'd like to propose a toast," she said. Glasses around the table rose in unison.

"Women don't make toasts," Calvin muttered at her elbow.

"This one does," Adriana said firmly.

"To my brother, Anthony Anderson," she said, "who dreamed a very big dream, and with the help of Felicia Ferantes..."

"Now Felicia Anderson," Tony interjected.

"Now Felicia Anderson," she continued, "has finally made that dream a reality. To Tony!" she sang out.

"To Tony!" they all joined in. Calvin was the last to make it to his feet, but he did make it. She smiled at him gratefully. Perhaps he'd accept them in time, she thought.

Tony tapped his glass and remained standing as the others took their seats. Adriana watched her brother struggle with his emotions. "Thank you," he said, his voice resonating with feeling. "And here's to friends and family... and life..."

Adriana exchanged worried glances with Felicia as Tony struggled for words, his eyes beginning to brim.

She knew Felicia longed to run to Tony, just as she did...

"And to the antipasto!" her brother exclaimed as the waiter set a magnificent tray of Italian delicacies in the center of the table.

The atmosphere exploded in cheers and applause, and Adriana looked above the white waiter's apron into the broad grin of Haines Scott. The gold flecks in his eyes seemed to dance across the table, mesmerizing her with their magnetism. She felt as though time had stopped, freezing the people, the scene, the noise around her, like some enchanted fairy-tale moment. She sat, lips parted, feeling her volition slip away. Here. In front of Calvin. How could she be letting it happen?

"Good evening," Scotty said, speaking, Adriana knew, to her alone. The words were quick, direct and honest, like his eyes. He was dressed in dark slacks and an open-necked white shirt, his sleeves rolled to the elbows, his coppery-gold hair curled and clung to his forearms, and escaped his shirt at the open collar.

Suddenly Adriana was aware that the table had hushed. All eyes turned, as if in slow motion, toward her and Scotty. Only Calvin seemed not to notice. Felicia's sisters smiled. Adriana barely caught the whispered phrase. It was Italian, something about thunder and lightning...

"This is my good friend, Haines Scott...Scotty." Tony's introduction broke the spell. "You know, of course, my wife...and Adriana."

"How does he happen to know you?" Calvin mumbled between bites of marinated mushroom.

"The kitchen, remember?" Adriana said, then held her breath.

"Um," Calvin nodded and speared another mushroom. Adriana sighed in relief. Calvin had been too busy eating to notice anything. Not that there was anything to notice, she told herself sternly. And not that it mattered. Calvin had his share of women friends.

Tony pulled up an extra chair across from Adriana and everyone made room at the table. "Let me get my jacket," Scotty said, turning toward the kitchen.

"The *waiter* is going to eat with us?" Calvin whispered behind his hand.

"Haines Scott is not a waiter," she heard herself say, a little too loudly. "He builds houses."

"And it's *Major* Haines Scott," Tony said distinctly. "He graduated from the U.S. Air Force Academy in astronautical engineering...with honors."

Adriana paused, a delicate green olive halfway to her lips. The Air Force Academy? So that's what he was doing in Colorado Springs. A space technician.

"But he can't cook as well as you can." Felicia's words interrupted Adriana's thoughts. She saw what Felicia knew. Tony had reached his simmering point. Calvin had a way of provoking him with just a word.

She saw that Calvin was interested. As Scotty returned and took his seat, Calvin rose and extended his hand across the table. "Calvin Caufield," he said with studied nonchalance. "I had a cousin at the academy. Class of '62."

Scotty took the proffered hand and shook it, his look registering intense concentration, thorough scrutiny. Adriana felt that in that one glance, he saw into Calvin's very soul.

"Sorry, but that was before my time—considerably." Scotty continued to shake Calvin's hand, but Adriana watched the older man's face pale slightly. She knew at that moment that Calvin Caufield had finally met his match.

She also knew that she needed to say something quickly. The two men stood, poised like bantam roosters ready for a cockfight. "What year did you graduate, Scotty?" she asked nervously.

He surveyed her for a long moment. With her eyes she begged him to be understanding. In his gaze she saw amusement, and a question. He took his time answering, almost seeming to enjoy her frustration. "I got the B.S. in 1971," he said, "then fooled around a bit before grad school at Columbia."

"Ha!" Tony roared. "Fooled around? Scotty logged a record number of missions flying F-4s in Vietnam. Won the top gun award twice." Adriana watched a look of genuine embarrassment pass across Scotty's face.

Then Lucio, Felicia's brother-in-law, known for rarely saying a word at family parties, rose and ceremoniously shook Scotty's hand. "I was a private in Nam," he said simply. She watched Scotty nod, accept the unspoken camaraderie with grace.

Beside her, Calvin bristled. Adriana knew he was searching for a way to bring up the war and his own political views. He would make it seem as though those who fought were to blame. He always did. "You've been pretty busy in your thirty-three years," she interjected hurriedly.

"Thirty-four," Scotty corrected.

"Of course—how could I forget? Scotty will be thirty-four on September twenty-third. It's the equinox. My birthday, too." Again, all eyes at the table were fastened on the two of them. She watched knowing smiles pass between family members. "You all must come and see the vases that Calvin gave me for my birthday," she added quickly. "They're beautiful."

"Valuable, too," Scotty added, his eyes holding hers. "Ming... right, Calvin?"

Adriana watched respect return to Calvin's face. Perhaps it would be all right after all, she thought. "You've seen the vases?" Calvin asked as he speared the last remaining marinated mushroom.

"Adriana showed them to me the night I took her the bed," Scotty answered with perfect equanimity.

"The *bed*?" Calvin asked. The mushroom dropped off his fork and plopped into his wineglass. Heads turned. Dead silence filled the room. Everyone waited for Scotty's response.

"We found a terrific buy on a brass bed Saturday. Didn't she tell you?" Adriana watched in fascinated horror as Scotty told the story of their purchase down to the last detail, including the farmer's joke. The group enjoyed the story immensely. Calvin sat in stony silence. She watched the tremble begin in his lower jaw. She should have told him about the bed. Scotty was not to blame. Or was he?

At that moment Angelo burst out of the kitchen with a flourish. "*Parmigeana di Melanzane*," he announced ceremoniously, setting the steaming dish of mozzarella-smothered eggplant before them. "And *Pollo a la Cacciatora*."

"It's a new dish," Tony explained. "Braised chicken cooked with black olives and anchovy sauce. One of Angelo's specialties."

"Tonight, cooked by this one!" Angelo's sweeping gesture indicated Scotty.

"Are you kidding?" Scotty said and colored. "You stood over me every minute." Everyone laughed and applauded good-naturedly. The dishes passed from hand to hand as the party began to eat with gusto. Felicia and her sisters left the table to fill the children's plates.

"Why would anyone want to learn to cook?" Calvin muttered, pushing the eggplant across his plate. Adriana watched her brother tense at the comment.

"It's creative," Scotty supplied. "Especially Italian cooking. You take the freshest, most perfect ingredients you can find—herbs, peppers, tomatoes..."

"*Good* tomatoes," Tony interjected. "We grow our own."

"And you mix them," Scotty continued, "just enough to create a blend of flavors." He paused then and looked from Calvin to Adriana and back again. "In Italian cooking, unlike French, the flavors do not lose their independence."

Calvin's eyes narrowed. "I still don't get it. To me, cooking is a chore. While I live alone I just endure it."

Scotty shrugged. "What else can I say?" he said. "It's creative. Like having children."

"That's something else I can do without," Calvin said, indicating the front dining room and the rising crescendo of children's voices. Adriana lowered her eyes, glad Felicia and her sisters were off with the children and had not heard Calvin's comment.

Tony cleared his throat. "Well, if I can make half the progress in the air that Scotty's made in the kitchen," Tony said, his voice low, "then we've struck an excellent bargain."

"In the air?" Calvin asked.

"Tony's going to learn to fly." Scotty's tones were guarded. "I'm teaching him."

"You're in for quite a challenge, fly-boy," Calvin said. "That man has not been in an airplane since he reached adulthood. I once suggested that he go to the fear of flying clinic in Boston, but he'd have to take an airplane to get there!"

Only Calvin enjoyed the joke. The tension in the room tightened. Adriana caught sight of Felicia, returning from the children's table, and hurried over to delay her. Over her shoulder, she heard Scotty's even tones. "He knows as much about aerodynamics as the average amateur pilot," he said, defending his friend. "He did extremely well in ground school."

When she returned to the table with Felicia, the tension had evaporated. Two bright spots of crimson still colored Tony's cheeks, but he was laughing now and pouring another round of Chianti for everyone. Scotty rose and pulled out her chair.

"What happened to Calvin?" she asked, indicating the empty seat, a corner of a crumpled napkin trailing in the sauce.

Scotty eyed her but she could not read his veiled expression. "Calvin said he had a big day tomorrow. He asked me if I'd mind seeing you home."

It was just like Calvin to disappear the moment he got bored, she thought. Adriana tried to muster sympathy and failed. Everyone seemed more relaxed now that Calvin had gone. He did have a way of putting a damper on parties. But now the warmth and affection flowed as freely as the red Chianti. Everyone seemed eager to show her they did not hold her responsible for Calvin's rudeness.

* * *

As Adriana stepped back, Scotty held her coat, his hands lingering on her shoulders. She saw Felicia's sisters nudge each other laughingly. Adriana blushed. This time she heard and understood. The "thunderbolt," an Italian word that meant love at first sight, the kind that was inescapable. They misunderstood, she thought with dismay. Abruptly she pulled away from Scotty and hurried to the parking lot.

"What's his middle name?" Scotty asked as he tucked her into the small car.

"Middle name?" she responded.

"Calvin," Scotty repeated, an edge of irritation in his voice. "What's his middle name?"

"Hugh," Adriana answered absently. She held on tightly as the car rumbled over the railroad tracks. He took the curves sharply, throwing her against him.

"Calvin Hugh Caufield." Scotty fairly spat out the words. "Adriana, do you have any idea what his name means?" She stared at him. Where was the anger coming from? Why was he turning on her like this? If anyone had a right to be angry, it was she herself. He hadn't yet apologized for his own rude behavior of the night before.

"'Hugh,' means 'mind,'" he stated matter-of-factly. "And 'Calvin' means 'bald.' Adriana, if you marry this guy, do you know what you'll be getting?" He braked hard in front of her house, slammed his own door and jerked hers open. She stood level with his flashing eyes, her own anger rising to meet his own. What right did he have to pass judgment on Calvin? Or on her decisions?

"You will be marrying a bald-headed intellectual snob," he stormed. "One who doesn't even like children." Adriana could not control her thoughts. They drifted to the thinning spot on Calvin's crown that he hid with careful combing. She hardly knew whether to laugh or cry, and so she mustered more anger.

"You can't judge a person by his name!" she shouted back. "And at least if I marry Calvin he won't drag me all over the countryside in a moving van."

Her words seemed to shock him in some unintelligible way. He tipped her face to him then, and brushed away the single tear she'd felt slide down her cheek. Adriana stared up into the troubled brown eyes, the gold flecks dulled within his gaze. He reached out and caught the hand she raised in its habitual gesture to her temple, then smoothed her hair himself. Adriana felt the tremble in his touch, felt her own heartbeat take off, racing to catch up with some elusive feeling she could not yet name. *Born for one another*. The Italian phrase rang in her ears as she watched him turn, stride down the walk and drive away.

Chapter Five

I've got the usual mix of fired-up freshmen," Adriana said, sliding quickly into the seat facing Calvin. The crowded loft above the student union cafeteria brimmed with noise, and Adriana nearly had to shout to make herself heard. "It's hard to believe so much anticipation and excitement can be crammed into one classroom. They're *bursting* with ideas." She bit ravenously into her sandwich and swallowed a gulp of iced tea.

"Don't eat so fast, Adriana. It's not good for your digestion." Calvin's tone was irritable. She watched him tap his cigarette impatiently. Gray ashes flew out of the small metal ashtray and settled on the bright orange Formica tabletop. She looked away. Out across the heads of the students below, through the two-story glass windows beyond, she rested her eyes on the distant forests of the Adirondack foothills shining green and golden in the sunlight. Calvin drummed his fingers on the tabletop.

"I have a one o'clock class, and it's scheduled all the way over in the Phys Ed complex," Adriana explained quickly. "I have to eat fast."

Calvin caught her wrist as she reached again for her glass. At his smooth, hot touch, Adriana felt perspiration gather in her palm. "I could talk to the chairman of the English Department," he said under his breath. "I'm sure they could move the class."

Adriana pulled her hand away. "Calvin, you know I'd never let you do that," she said. "I can fight my own battles with the administration. And anyway, I know I'll like that class. The athletes will have to drop if the room is moved. Some of them have had a rough time with English. They're going to be a real challenge..." Adriana let her voice trail off as Calvin shrugged. As he bent over his own sandwich, her gaze fell inadvertently on the thinning hair atop his head.

"If you want a real challenge, finish your Ph.D. Then you'll be teaching upperclassmen exclusively, Adriana."

"A bald-headed intellectual snob." Scotty's epithets scraped across her memory. Adriana cringed. She wanted to fight someone, anyone, to prove that Calvin wasn't what he seemed. Instead, she raised her hand to brush her hair off her temple, and in a rush of feeling remembered Scotty's touch. "Calvin, can't you remember how it was to be a freshman?" she blurted out.

Ignoring her question, Calvin countered with his own. "How late were you out last night? I trust Tony got you home at a reasonable hour?"

"Haines Scott took me home," she snapped. "It was early. The party broke up shortly after you left." She watched his face for even the slightest hint of jealousy, but he simply hurried on.

"Speaking of parties, Mother wants us to come for lunch next Saturday afternoon. Pick you up about ten?"

"Sure, of course," she said mechanically.

"It's almost one," Calvin reminded her. "You'd better run."

Three hours and two classes later, Adriana unlocked the door of her office. She tossed the heavy briefcase crammed with sample themes on the desk top. Tuesday-Thursday classes would be a bit grueling at first, she knew, because of the extra half-hour length of each class. And she still had to face the evening class at the base. Adriana slumped tiredly into her chair, kicked off her shoes and propped her stocking feet up on an unpacked carton of books.

The small barren office felt stuffy and Adriana leaned over to pull the drapes and tilt open the window. Warm air and sunlight spread across her lap and settled in the empty bookshelves around her. She'd worked hard for this moment, she thought, settling back in the chair. Now she had two places to call home, the old Victorian in Rome and this small office on the campus of Utica College.

Adriana gazed out onto the grassy quadrangle beyond the window. In the shadow of the bronze sculpture of mother and child, a young man lay stretched on the grass, his head in the lap of a blond-haired coed. Adriana caught the masculine chuckle as the girl tickled his nose with a late-blooming dandelion. She'd missed moments like that. Calvin had never been... playful.

Adriana closed her eyes quickly. When she opened them, she focused slowly. I'm more tired than I realized, she thought, rubbing her eyes against the blur on the window. No, she saw suddenly, it wasn't a blur, but a large butterfly, its wings splayed against the outside of the glass.

Adriana watched the insect fan itself in the sunlight and thought again of Haines Scott. Would butterflies forever remind her of that man?

She rose and began to unpack her books and stack them on the shelves, sorting them by periods: Victorian, Renaissance, Medieval. In her mind she continued to sort the bits of Scotty's life she'd collected thus far. She wondered at the incongruities. He was suited, she knew, to the woods, old houses and even the small town familiarity of Tony's restaurant. How could he possibly be connected to the vagabond life of the U.S. Air Force? He belonged in Rome...and in her life...somewhere. Where?

She looked again out the window at the couple, joined now by other young men and women. Her own classmates had come and gone, but that had never prevented her from feeling close to many of them. Why not to Scotty? He was sure to be reassigned soon. But now counted, too. Still the monarch clung to her window. She watched the insect, savoring its beauty until it caught a breeze and fluttered away.

She'd stayed too long. The campus traffic clogged Burrstone Road and then fed slowly into the four lanes of Highway 49, slowing the Utica-Rome commuter route to a crawl. There wouldn't be time to stop at home for dinner. She'd have to settle for something from the snack machine at the base's educational building's lounge. She'd plan better next week.

Reaching the Skyline Gate of Griffiss Air Force Base at last, Adriana slowed, rolled up to the guardhouse and waited. She tried not to think of the thousand and one times she'd sped through that gate in her father's car, the guardsman stepping aside and saluting smartly. And that one last time. The low, black funeral limousine had crept through the gate, turned left at Kirkland Drive, inched toward the chapel.

She came close to mumbling some excuse. She could always call off sick, even cancel the class. No. She wanted to teach this class more than any other. It was in her own field, her first love. Fantasy literature. Despite her fatigue and hunger and the ache left in her heart at even the sight of the air base, Adriana felt her excitement mount.

She saw him before he saw her. He sat in the back of the classroom, his long legs stretched out before him as he sorted through the pile of paperbacks assigned for the class. He looked for all the world like all the graduate students she'd gone to school with.

Except for the flight suit. He must have come directly from a mission. She half expected to hear jets screaming overhead. "You don't just get into those planes," she'd heard her father say, "you put them on." There was no denying it. He was a flyer. He belonged to the U.S. Air Force first. Anyone or anything else would run a remote second. Adriana felt the last of her illusions slip away as two other students came into the room, saw Scotty and saluted. He raised his eyes to acknowledge them. And then he saw her.

She couldn't read the mixture of emotions that fought their way across his face. So he hadn't known she would be the instructor? *Of course not.* The schedule had said "staff." *But perhaps he'd asked.* He knew she was teaching a class at the base. *No.* She already knew him well enough to recognize his streak of insatiable curiosity. It would be just like him to sign up for a course in fantasy literature. And life in Rome meant always bumping into someone you knew.

Still, it unnerved her to be standing here in front of him. Whatever he'd been feeling was under control now. She stood self-consciously, seeing herself through his eyes. His leisurely glance swept up her high-heeled suede boots and visually smoothed the folds of her camel-colored skirt. At the soft cashmere sweater, his eyes paused and lingered, and Adriana felt herself blush to match its crimson color.

Two more uniformed men entered the room, saluted and paused to shake hands. The spell was broken. Adriana busied herself with her notes, but she did not miss the extra measure of respect the two men paid Scotty. It was more than rank. She'd have to ask Tony about it.

Tony? It was her first thought of him all day and he'd planned to go flying this morning. But of course Scotty would know how the lesson had gone. She'd ask him at break.

Adriana passed out the syllabus, explained the requirements and direction of the course and answered questions. It was all she could do to avoid Scotty's eyes, but she failed only once.

"Anyone who chooses may substitute an original work of fiction for the term paper," she directed. The gold flecks in Scotty's eyes came alive and nearly jumped out at her.

"Have you tried to write before?" she asked him later between hungry bites of the apple she'd gotten from the snack machine.

She watched him pause to think. She wouldn't have been at all surprised to hear he was a writer. He'd certainly done just about everything else.

"Only limericks," he said at last, the teasing look crinkling the corners of his eyes. "There was a young teacher from Rome," he began, "who never could find her way home..."

"That's enough," Adriana said and laughed. "There's no telling where that might lead."

"I was hoping it would lead to dinner after class," he said. "I'm starving."

"Me too," she said before she thought. It was a date. Undeniably. She thought fleetingly of Calvin and felt something close to guilt, "I wanted to ask you how it went with Tony, too," she added hastily.

Scotty's eyes warmed with concern. "I'll tell you all about it after class," he said.

After the break, Adriana gave a short writing assignment in which each student was to outline his own definition of fantasy. From the back of the room Scotty's smile flashed, unmistakably sensual. She had visions of his finished limerick. "*Literary* fantasy," she explained. Masculine chuckles filled the room. Adriana laughed along with them. She'd have to remember that this class was made up of mainly unattached, very eligible bachelors, none of whom knew that she didn't date...exactly. Especially not transient air force personnel...usually.

An hour later, Scotty was dumping his armload of paperbacks and her bulging briefcase into the back of the Sprite. Adriana stared at the clutter of their belongings, her camel-colored cardigan tangled in his leather flight jacket, his books mixed with hers. She felt hungry and very tired, but something about the tangled mass tugged at her imagination. Then Scotty's arm brushed hers, sending unexpected waves of excitement through her body. He opened the door, helped her in, located her seat belt. Was she giving herself over to Scotty's control? Risking something foolish?

"I think—" he seemed to continue her thoughts rather than interrupt them, as though their minds flowed uncontrollably into one another "—I think we both need to relax."

She watched the strong suntanned hands grasp the gearshift, move it confidently into place, flip the ignition with a practiced motion. Adriana transposed those hands to the controls of a fighter, struggling to remind herself of the wall between them. "The officers' club has a late buffet," he was saying: "There will be something hot . . . drinks . . . a little quiet music."

Why had she said yes? Why had he asked? Hadn't they both made it perfectly clear to each other that neither had intentions of anything beyond friendship?

Moments later they were dancing. She had to think. What was it they had said last night on her porch? What was it she had decided today in her office? Something about butterflies. Scotty pulled her closer. Warm. Protective. And dangerous, a corner of her tired mind warned her. But his chest felt firm, just as she'd imagined it would feel. His right hand, splayed against her lower back, pressed ever so gently, reminding her of the butterfly pressed against her office window.

It was so...comfortable, she thought, relaxing into his arms. And after all, what harm could possibly come of it? Her life was set—her home, her job, real roots for the first time in her life, and Calvin, possibly, if they could . . . adjust to one another.

Scotty's hand drew hers closer to his heart, brushing the rise of her breasts. Adriana shivered. He responded instantly by drawing her closer, close enough to kiss the top of her ear through her tangled hair. The warmth of his breath seemed to shoot through her, bringing Adriana instantly to her senses.

"Let's get something to eat," he whispered before she had had a chance to respond to the challenge of his kiss. Adriana was not at all sure she still felt hungry. Nor was she certain she could stand long enough to move through the buffet line. Her knees felt like jelly. She leaned on Scotty for support.

"Sit down," he insisted, steering her toward a table near the circular fireplace. "You're more tired than you realize. I'll bring you a plate." She watched him move across the room toward the buffet table. He was right. She was just very tired, nothing more.

"You were going to tell me about Tony," Adriana reminded Scotty as he set a plate of steamed shellfish before her. He didn't answer immediately. She watched him slowly, methodically, spread butter on her roll and his own. No one, Adriana was certain, had ever buttered a roll for her. She watched him, mesmerized.

"It's going to take a little longer than I thought," he said at last. "I couldn't get him into the plane today." Adriana listened intently. "I thought that his success in ground school would provide momentum," Scotty went on. "He ought to have been ready to taxi today, but last night . . . slowed him up a bit."

"Calvin's comment?" she asked quietly. Scotty did not answer. "Sometimes Calvin speaks before he thinks," Adriana said, more to herself than to Scotty. "He doesn't really mean to be unkind."

"It doesn't much matter, does it? Tony believed him. It's going to be a while before he goes near the airstrip again."

"Oh, good grief!" she exploded. "Why can't Tony just listen to common sense. The crash was an accident. I keep telling him that fate won't waste a whole airplane full of innocent people just to get even with him. That's egotistical." Her eyes flashed into Scotty's, the fury settling there and cooling. He knew her anger was really directed against Calvin. "Maybe there's nothing to do but wait it out," she added softly.

"I don't think so, Adriana. He's got to keep trying. If we can just get him up once, I think he'll be okay."

He dropped her later at her car, waiting while she started the engine. She lingered, thanked him for dinner, then finally headed out of the empty parking lot, leaving him still standing, his long, lanky body draped over the canvas top of the Sprite, watching her.

She was fumbling with the house key when she heard his car pull up in front. She spun, surprised, and saw him wave her briefcase cheerfully as he climbed out of the small car. He jogged easily up the walk and joined her on the porch.

"Some women use the darnedest excuses," he said softly. "If you wanted me to come for coffee, all you had to do was ask."

"I can't make coffee," Adriana answered. "All I have is instant."

"Just what I had in mind," he said, taking her keys and opening the door. She tried to protest, or think about protesting. But excuses would not form in her mind. He held the door for her and she followed him inside, pausing in the study to drop her heavy briefcase on the cluttered desk. Absently she began to empty it.

His hands on her shoulders startled her. Why was it, she thought in irritation, that his touch unnerved her so? He was only helping her off with her cardigan. As he reached to lay her wrap across the desk chair, one hand remained loosely on her shoulder. Her fingers trembled as she continued to stack and restack the contents of her briefcase.

His hands slid down her shoulders. Loosely he clasped her waist and pulled her back against his chest. Again she felt the warmth of his breath in her hair and on her neck. It seemed to reach inside her, fanning the white-hot ember of desire until it lapped like wildfire at her heart.

"I wanted a chance to tell you," he was saying. "I won't push you, Adriana. You were right about what you said last night. I don't have much to offer, I . . ." He had turned her then, in his arms, and she knew he saw the heat that seemed to be consuming her.

Scotty's mouth came down hard on hers. Her half-formed protest became an invitation as the kiss deepened, and he moved his lips down her arched throat. He was sitting now on the edge of the cot, the small room full of him and her and the fire between them. His hands slid up, beneath her sweater, finding the curve of her breasts.

"Scotty...?" she moaned as she slid down beside him, allowed him to unfasten the front clasp of her bra.

"I don't know," he groaned in response. "I only know...I knew you'd look like this..." He smoothed his hands across her heaving breasts. She watched, wide-eyed, marveling at the sensual brush of his sun-tanned touch across her olive skin, the gentle massaging movement of his thumbs across her dark brown nipples.

He caressed her slowly, gently, kissing the valley of her breasts, their full, ripe swell, the nipples now peaked in tense excitement. She arched into him, leaning into his mouth, pulling him to herself.

One by one he loosened articles of her clothing. Like remnants of a shed cocoon, they fell, a tangled mass on the floor beside the small cot. Adriana clung as she had never clung in her life, to this man and to the wild, hungry feeling that he had brought to birth in her.

Outside, the wind began to blow, sending dry leaves scraping across the porch. Scotty paused, pressed her to himself and seemed to listen to the sound as though it carried some distant warning. Adriana began to tremble in his arms.

Gently, he placed her in the small cot and tucked the covers in around her. He turned off the light and then sat down on the edge of the cot, her hand in his, moonlight bathing the room and settling in his eyes. Soft brown, liquid as spun honey, they feasted on her face. Adriana felt a shadow pass across her heart as it passed across his face, tugging her toward reality. She parted her lips to speak.

"No," he hushed her. "We won't talk about it now. I have to go to Edwards tomorrow...today," he added, glancing at his watch. "We'll talk on the weekend when I get back."

He was gone before Adriana could respond. She lay listening to the sound of the Sprite as it faded into the stillness of the evening. She'd known him barely a week and every day had ended with his leaving. Adriana turned her face to the wall and cried.

Chapter Six

She settled into the familiar comfort of Calvin's blue Mercedes and tugged at her seat belt. Beyond the tinted glass of the car windows the day sparkled in sharp, cool clarity, but inside the car the air was hot. Adriana drew shallow, hurried breaths.

It had been that way all week. She had rushed from one class to another, fallen exhausted into bed every night, lost all track of time. On top of everything she'd forgotten to cancel lunch with Calvin and his mother. She had fully intended to do so. It had been her first thought Wednesday morning. Almost her first thought.

Scotty hadn't called. Not even a note. Not that it mattered. Wasn't he the great American heart-breaker? Tony had said so. She should have known. Besides, she'd had her life all worked out. Permanence. Roots. Those were the things that mattered, the things that kept life whole. It had been simply a moment of abandon. Neither of them had intended it. Haines Scott was everything she'd vowed to avoid in life. And Calvin? Adriana didn't want to think about it.

"I'll have the air conditioner going in just a moment," Calvin said. She watched him mop the moisture from his forehead, then fumble at the ignition. For a moment she considered feigning illness. Anything to escape the afternoon ahead. Or she could tell him outright, now, this very instant. *I'm falling in love with Haines Scott, Calvin,* she'd rehearsed. *So?* she heard him answer in her mind.

"We could put the windows down," Adriana suggested. "Why not take the back roads through the country. I saw some butterflies last week—"

"You know my hay fever," Calvin interrupted. He swung the car toward the New York State Thruway.

Adriana felt a small knot of anger form in her throat. She knew she couldn't argue. She'd seen Calvin often enough, eyes watering, nose dripping. *In sickness and in health*. The words skipped across her conscience. Was it the price one paid for certainty, stability? Did Haines Scott suffer from hay fever? She erased the thought before it could gain a foothold and began to recount her first week of classes.

Calvin listened, absently she knew, then launched into a discussion of his trip to Greece and his research project. Adriana had long ago learned all she ever cared to know about Greek amphoras. At last they turned up the large circular drive of the austere Federalist-style mansion on a hill overlooking Syracuse University.

Calvin's mother was waiting for them. "How nice!" The heavily jeweled fingers clutched at Adriana, drawing her into the foyer. "I'm so delighted you finally found a moment to drop by." The older woman smiled condescendingly. *If only it could be just a moment,* Adriana sighed to herself as Calvin bent to kiss his mother's heavily powdered upturned cheek.

"I was just telling Adriana about my trip, Mother. And I've brought the slides."

"You should have told me they were ready! You know my friends are dying to see them. I'll have Henri set up the projector in the library." The old woman went off to find her houseman, her heels clicking on the polished floor of the entryway. The hollow sound reverberated, reminding Adriana of her own bare floors and empty rooms. Maybe rugs won't solve the problem, she thought, eyeing the thick Oriental carpets in the library to her right and in the living room to her left.

Adriana left Calvin in the library busily sorting slides and went off to the kitchen, partly to visit Francine and partly just to escape to a sunny room. As Calvin did in his brownstone in Utica, Mrs. Caufield kept the drapes drawn night and day for fear a stray wisp of sunlight would fade or warp some priceless piece of furniture or bric-a-brac.

"Mmm, asparagus soup." Adriana stirred the simmering mixture. "You're such a good cook, Francine."

"I hope you'll remember that, Miss Anderson," the plump woman whispered. "Someday me and Henri would like to work for you . . . and Mr. Calvin."

"Mrs. Caufield would never give you up, Francine. And I can no more imagine having live-in help, even as friendly and wonderful as you and Henri, than I can imagine lunch every day off antique dishes."

Adriana followed Francine into the dining room and carefully placed the cranberry luncheon plates on the white damask cloth.

"Adriana, don't trouble yourself." Mrs. Caufield breezed in from the library. "Let Francine do that. Come here, there's something I want to talk to you about."

She followed the older woman across the hallway and into the massive formal living room. Adriana shuddered, remembering the afternoons she'd reluctantly left her books in the basement to pour tea or serve finger sandwiches. Only the weekends in Rome had saved her grades and her sanity.

"I want to show you my new grandnephew," Mrs. Caufield said, leading the way to an array of formal portraits arranged atop a baby grand piano.

Adriana accepted the heavy gilt frame and looked into the usual chubby face of a tiny infant. "The baby is quite attractive," the old woman stated, "but he'll grow up to look just like his father. I can't abide that man." Adriana had heard the story innumerable times. She'd finally decided that the grudge the old woman bore was based solely on Calvin's cousin's vocation. He was a doctor. Mrs. Caufield's greatest disappointment in life had been that Calvin had hated medicine.

"I want you to be very firm with him," Mrs. Caufield was continuing. "Tell Calvin you won't marry him unless he lets you have children. That's why you've been avoiding the issue, isn't it? He's going to ask you soon," the old woman assured her. "I've already had Grandmother Caufield's diamond reset."

Adriana stared at the old woman. Suddenly the air in the living room seemed as hot and stuffy as Calvin's car. "But you know he doesn't want children," she said. "We've discussed it. He's dead set."

"Well, then—" the old woman lowered her voice to a whisper "—you'll just have to trick him. Women do it all the time. He'll come around once he finds he has a son."

Adriana felt as though the room had suddenly gone cold. "I doubt that seriously," she said, replacing the framed picture on the piano.

"Well, I won't have everything I own going to Holton Caufield's child!" The old woman's voice trembled with barely contained fury. "And don't worry, you won't have to give up your teaching career. I'll bring Francine and Henri to Utica when I come."

"You're moving to Utica?" Adriana asked in surprise.

"Didn't Calvin tell you?" the old woman asked. "It's silly to keep both houses, and of course the Utica brownstone has been in the family for generations. We only moved here in the sixties because Calvin's father accepted the Sherman Chair at Syracuse. It's time I went back. My roots are all in Utica. And I've kept up my country club membership."

Roots. Adriana had mulled over the meaning of the word in her old basement room as she'd packed up her few remaining books. Tony, Felicia and the children entwined with images of Calvin's house in Utica. And a child of her own? Adriana had felt her heart jump. She might just get Calvin to agree. The feeling had passed as quickly as it had come. Adriana knew that Calvin would never really want the child. And babies weren't something one had in order to stave off grasping relatives. Besides, Mrs. Caufield was wrong on another count. It wasn't Calvin's feeling about children that had her sidestepping his proposals. There were other things. *Scotty? No.* Lots of other things. Tony was right. She didn't owe Calvin anything. She had grown out of needing the security he offered....

The asparagus soup was not as good as she remembered, and after lunch Adriana found herself dozing through Calvin's slides.

"I thought you were interested in this project," he said accusingly on the way home.

Adriana stared out the window into the gathering darkness. "It's just been a difficult week, Calvin. I'm tired."

"Well, I hope you're not too tired to hear me out, Adriana," he said, almost formally. "There's something I'd like to discuss with you." She knew without asking what it was. *I'm not ready,* her thoughts screamed as Calvin pulled up in front of her house.

Adriana hurried up the walk as Calvin unloaded the box of books from the Mercedes. Halfway up the steps she cried out in surprise as a tall figure moved out of the shadows and approached her.

"It's only me." She recognized the confident voice of Haines Scott and looked up into brown-gold eyes rimmed with fatigue and not a little irritation. "I forgot my key," he said as Calvin approached.

"You really should get that watchdog," Calvin mumbled, laboring up the steps with the box. "Forgot your key?" He looked blankly from Adriana to Scotty and back again.

Was he trying to make Calvin jealous? she wondered. He didn't know Calvin very well or he'd never have tried. And why was he so irritable? Did he expect she'd just sit home waiting till he decided to call?

"Scotty is doing the kitchen, remember?" she said to Calvin, a little more crisply than she'd intended.

"Not today, I'm not," Scotty shot back. "It's a little late to start the measuring. And I've got to be on base in an hour."

"That's okay," she answered coolly. "I'm really exhausted. We'll talk another time," she added, turning to Calvin. "I wouldn't be able to concentrate—"

"I've got the faculty coffee tomorrow," Calvin interrupted. "And appointments all next week... Maybe Friday?"

Adriana looked from one man to the other. Scotty towered over her, his hands thrust in the pockets of his worn leather flight jacket. The fading light reflected off the air force insignia on the hat that shadowed his expression. Calvin, meanwhile, impatiently shifted the box of books from one arm to another. Ignoring them both, Adriana turned to unlock the door.

"See you around," Scotty said and swung his long legs off the porch. He was halfway down the walk by the time she remembered their agreement to "talk" when he'd returned from Edwards. His long strides carried him away so quickly, she thought.

Adriana blinked into the blinding Sunday morning sunlight streaming in through the half-open front door. In the chilly air she clutched her thin blouse tightly under her chin. From Scotty's arms, a small furry mass of wriggling rusty-colored energy bounded free, landed at her feet and began to chew the laces of her sneaker.

"Calvin said you needed protection." Adriana looked into the gold-brown eyes of the man who had continued to haunt her dreams. "Forgiven?" he asked.

She stood speechless. So it had been as she suspected. A moment's lapse. Both of them giving in to something primal, something neither of them had really wanted.

"Look, I promise to...respect Calvin's cause...in every way. But I don't want to let Tony, or you, down. I've got the stuff in the truck to start the kitchen."

She would not let him know that he was wrong, that he'd only reached out and touched what she herself had offered. She ought to be asking him to forgive her. Adriana bent down and scooped up the tiny puppy. It tried to wriggle up her arms and nuzzle her chin. She laughed then. Scotty laughed, too, the rich sound of his voice tangling in her own. She looked up into the brown-gold eyes brimming with unspoken need, felt her own eyes respond. She'd have to learn to look somewhere above them, she thought, her gaze moving up to tangle in the coppery mass of hair.

"I was just putting the kettle on for a pot of tea," she said. "Shall we start with that?" He nodded and she held the door for him. The tiny dog shivered in her arms and Adriana hugged him close to still her own trembling.

"I'll block off the laundry room behind the kitchen," she said. "It's warm in there and he'll hear you working. I've got to prepare for next week's classes. And I've made up a pretty strict schedule for finishing my thesis. I don't know how much help I can be today. . . or in the future."

"No problem," he said lightly.

They sat at the kitchen table, hands cupped around their steaming mugs. She settled back, comforted somehow by his presence and then, before she realized what was happening, she was telling him about her latest story.

"Fantasy?" he asked.

"Yes," she answered. "They're all some sort of fantasy. I don't know where it comes from, but even stories that don't start out that way get bent somewhere along the line."

"Why do you suppose that happens?" He stared at her so intently that she had to look away. She took two spoonfuls from the small pewter sugar bowl, dumped them in her tea and stirred thoughtfully.

"Funny," she mused. "It has something to do with reality. In ordinary life, real things, real feelings, are so difficult to describe. But build a fantasy world, a world where one thing, however small is, well, *strange* and all of a sudden that's when it's easy to see the shape of things, to decide what's important, what's lasting, valuable. It's hard to explain."

Scotty nodded. "I think I know the feeling," he said. "When I'm flying thousands of miles above the earth looking down at nothing but a patch of blue-green with only the instruments to guide me, it's then that I feel almost certain of where home is, most tied to it."

He said the word "home" with a poignancy that made her pause, lay the silver spoon aside, half reaching toward his hand. "And where is 'home,' Scotty?" She tried to sound nonchalant. "Colorado?"

"No. Maybe. I don't know. Once I was certain it was Portland. Adriana, you ought to see the house I built there..." He paused midsentence, and she watched the troubled expression return and move across his face, obscuring it until she lost the feeling of knowing what he meant. He shrugged as though giving up on the idea himself.

Adriana rose, rinsed her cup and his. She found a little bowl and gave the puppy water. "There's some puppy chow in the truck. I'll bring it in later," Scotty said. "Be careful not to feed him too much, just regularly. He'll take anything you offer... he'll be fat in no time."

She brought a shallow cardboard box from the basement and folded an old blanket into it. The puppy promptly climbed inside and fell asleep.

"Better put some papers down, too," Scotty advised. "He looks like he's going to make himself right at home."

"Speaking of being right at home," Adriana said, busily spreading the papers, "I'd better give you a key." She would not mention last night's episode, she decided. Their mutual positions were clear now. She fished in the small toolbox under the sink and pulled out an old-fashioned latch key. "It's to the side door," she explained. "It will be easier if you bring things in that way, I think."

He took the key from her, dropped it in his pocket and stood. "I'd better get busy," he said. "By the way... Adriana..." He turned, leaned into the oak doorjamb, his sturdy outline framed against the sunlit hall beyond, the random copper-colored strands glowing like wildfire in his hair.

She felt her pulse quicken at the sight of him and at the sound of her name on his lips. "What is it, Scotty?"

Too late. He'd caught the impulse. It seemed to travel the length of the room and draw him closer. She watched him lean away from the door and move a step toward her. Was it the way he had said her name? Enunciating each syllable as if the sounds had taste? Or the way she said his, tripping it lightly off her own tongue? Adriana knew her nature was slow, controlled—"earthy," her mother had called it. But now, just saying his name filled her with urgency, brought back all the desire she'd felt when he'd touched her. Adriana willed her heart to stillness.

"Scotty?" she said again, to test herself.

She watched him collect himself, square the broad shoulders, brush a suntanned hand through his hair. "Nothing," he answered. "Just that I hope I can finish. I'm not sure how much time..."

"Don't worry about it," she answered. "I'm grateful to have any help you can give me."

He nodded and went out to unload the rest of his supplies. Adriana returned to the study. She heard him at the side entrance, then later the whir of a saw from the kitchen. The sounds faded as she became engrossed in her work.

She hadn't heard him come in, only smelled the tantalizing aroma of the bacon, lettuce and tomato sandwich moments before he set it down in front of her. She stretched, rubbed her neck, glanced quickly at her watch. "Close to 2:00 p.m.," she said. "I can't believe it!" She rubbed her neck again.

"Once you get started you really get into it," he said. "Let me work on that for a while." Before she could protest, he had moved behind her chair, his fingers working the tired muscles of her neck. "I used to do this for my mother," he said. "She said it helped her migraines."

"Migraines?" Adriana mused. The exquisitely practiced fingers paused momentarily, then continued the steady massage.

"Among other things," he answered distantly. "She hasn't been well for some time. You'd better eat your sandwich before it gets cold."

Adriana sighed as he withdrew his fingers. The warm, tingling spot on her neck moved down her back to relax her entire being. Touching, she mused, she was so hungry for it. Wasn't everyone? She thought of Calvin's self-assured disdain for couples who "hung on each other."

"I'm sorry," she said quickly. "I should have made lunch for you."

"Why? I thought we agreed you don't cook."

"Ha!" she said. "Even I can fry bacon!"

"Come on," he said suddenly. "If we're going to talk cooking we need to be in the kitchen." She eyed her books and papers. "Fifteen minutes?" he said. "You do have to eat."

She carried the sandwich and followed him, pausing to break off a tiny piece of her bacon for the dog.

"Better watch that," he said, his voice a note lower. "He'll take anything you offer." She rose to look directly into Scotty's brown-gold eyes. The wide grin that spread across his face told her he'd read her thought.

Quickly she turned toward the kitchen table. He moved a heavy tape measure and turned over a drawing. "Have you ever seen what a microwave can do for bacon?" he asked her.

"Felicia has one," she said. "She swears by it."

"It's exactly what you need, Adriana. It's a great time-saver and since you're just learning to cook, you'll adapt easily. And look, you've got a perfect place for it." He led her to the far side of the kitchen opposite the dining room door. She stood, gazing out the eye-level window, watching yellow-red maple leaves fall into the yard next door.

"We'll extend the cabinet under the window," he continued. "The microwave will fit perfectly. Every time you use it you can stand and look outside, just as you're doing now."

"Have you got any idea what's on my list of things to buy, after fixing the wiring, of course? Where do you get these ideas, Scotty?"

"From you, of course," he said simply. "The kitchen has to suit you." He was standing too close, she thought. If she could just keep him from standing quite so close... She pushed back her hair. Their elbows bumped and they both exploded in laughter. Something new, and safer, had started between them. Adriana was sure they would be friends.

"I've got to be going," he said finally. His voice slid along easily like water over smooth rock.

"Of course," she said. She wondered if the reluctance in her voice was too suggestive.

"Think of a name," he said over his shoulder.

"A name?"

"For the pup." He paused, his hand on the doorknob, his back to her.

Adriana waited, holding her breath, but he neither turned nor spoke again. A chill swept through the room as he opened the door and left.

She tidied the kitchen, then played awhile with the puppy. He'd knocked over the wastebasket and was attacking the bright blue strip of foil from a tin of biscuits. "Biscuit," she decided. "I'll call you Biscuit, because your first home is off the kitchen and your first toy is a biscuit wrapper. And you're just the color of a little, fat, oven-browned biscuit."

Adriana settled the dog in his bed and returned to her work in the study. Words seemed to hang in the air, refusing to settle on the page. She kept seeing Scotty, framed in the doorway of her home.

October passed much as September had. Adriana taught, wrote, traveled the Utica-Rome road daily, watching the leaves change, fall and scatter in the frozen weeds along the roadside. Scotty was there, always in the background, mostly on weekends, shoving sandwiches under her nose or calling her to hold a piece of molding in place. Sometimes he'd leave her notes when he'd come to work and find her out with Calvin. But they were simple messages. She soon came to expect nothing more than honesty in his brown-gold eyes.

He'd taken Biscuit for his shots, and the pup was big enough now to climb the stairs and snuggle at the foot of her bed. And she'd gone ahead and bought the microwave and surprised him one evening with chicken tarragon and green salad. The wiring and the rugs could wait, she had decided.

They fell into a habit of dinner together Tuesdays after class, sometimes stopping in at Tony's after he'd closed up. Over leftover spaghetti or maybe ravioli, Scotty asked innumerable questions about the assigned book. Adriana answered patiently, marveling, as always, over his insatiable curiosity. When Felicia called from the house across the garden, Tony would insist they stay and just lock up on their way out.

"You've got to get on the stick, Tony," Scotty would chide gently. "We've got to get you off the ground before your license lapses."

"I've been busy with the restaurant," Tony hedged.

What had Calvin said that had upset him so? Adriana wondered. Calvin. He was always at the fringe of her life—the note on her door the day she'd gone with Scotty to pick up the new sink and cabinets, the plant he'd sent to her office after she was settled—what matter that it was a cactus, the idea counted, didn't it? Occasionally they lunched together on campus between classes. Or she sat in the library reading while he burrowed through the archives.

"Your mother said she's thinking of moving to Utica," Adriana said one day over sandwiches. "I suppose that means we would live in my house in Rome..."

Calvin stirred his coffee, sloshing the liquid carelessly onto the table. Since he didn't bother to mop up, she took her napkin and did it for him. The coarse white paper drank the dismal brown liquid greedily.

"The brownstone is huge," Calvin said. She watched his eyes dart furtively around the room, lightly, like nervous houseflies, to the young women seated around them, refusing to meet her own. "You know that when I get to be dean I'll have to do a lot of entertaining."

"My living room is large enough," she supplied quickly. "I don't have a lot of furniture yet, but when I have a chance..."

"Adriana, most of the faculty lives in Utica. You know that. We can't ask them to drive all the way to Rome for functions."

"I drive it every day," she said. "It's less than half an hour."

Calvin's expression changed to annoyance. "Just wait till the dead of winter, Adriana. You've lived here long enough to know why they call this area 'the snow belt.' And I've heard we're due for our first storm any day."

She stared across the table at Calvin. Why had she ever thought he would give up a home he'd had in the family for three generations? And what was the matter with her, anyway? Couldn't she move, just half an hour away, for a man who'd share her life forever? Forever. It seemed a word wrought out of iron, not at all pleasant, hardly comforting.

"Adriana," he was saying, his hand reaching toward hers. "You know I've wanted to talk to you about this very subject. I know I've been busy on the journal article. And you've been busy on your thesis. But what about Thanksgiving? Can you be back from your aunt's house by Saturday? Mother's expecting us, you know."

"I'll try, Calvin," she answered, hoping to check the tremble in his chin before it could start. She ought to have told him long ago. She'd never marry him. She knew that now. Why had she let it drag on and on?

Chapter Seven

Scotty frowned at her over coffee the day the furnace first kicked on and the lights dimmed. "That's it," he said. "I'm going to talk to a guy I know on the base, get him over here to see what's going on."

"I don't use the furnace all that much, anyway," Adriana answered. "The fireplace heats the whole downstairs and I sleep under tons of blankets."

"Um," said Scotty. "I'll bet you do."

She punched him good-naturedly from across the table. He caught her doubled fist and squeezed gently. And she watched the familiar feeling rise in his gold-brown eyes. But this time, instead of fading into anonymity, it lingered, and drew her into his field of vision. She felt as though his eyes saw through her, through her clothes, saw every inch of her warming, naked skin. Adriana felt the fire of the golden flecks lick her own dormant emotions into white-hot frenzy. She'd been a fool to think she'd grown immune to it, crazy to believe she could ever look, *really look*, at him again without risking her very soul. And she could not escape the feeling that it was, perhaps, a risk she was doomed to take.

Adriana pulled her hand away and reached for the empty coffee cups. Rising quickly, she carried them to the sink. "Let's forget work for an afternoon," she said impetuously. "They've flooded the tennis courts down the street. You said you hadn't skated in years. Now's your chance."

"Why not?" he said, pulling the plug on the drill. Adriana watched, distracted, as he wound the long cord in loops along his forearm. The muscles in his shoulders flexed smoothly beneath the snug knit turtleneck. How she longed to touch him there, to feel his latent animal strength.

"I said, have you got any idea where I can borrow skates?" he asked, repeating the question she'd not heard.

"The family next door had six boys when I last counted," she said. "They're bound to have some extra skates."

She was pulling on her leg warmers when the phone rang. "Tony, hello! Sure, he's here. Just a minute." Adriana passed the phone to Scotty and left to hunt for her heavy mittens.

"Adriana!" Even from the back of the closet she could not miss the exuberance in his voice. "Adriana, he's ready! Where the hell are you?"

"Hall closet," she called, searching one last time for the elusive mate to her old rabbit fur mitten. Scotty pushed aside the bulky winter coats, knocking over two umbrellas and a broom. The brush attachment to the vacuum cleaner toppled off the shelf and bounced into her lap. Adriana looked up, grinning.

"A girl can't get away from you even in the privacy of her own hall closet," she said, pretending chagrin. "Are you trying to get my attention or something?"

Scotty laughed, offered his hand to help her up. She pulled hard and he lost his balance. "Help me find this mitten, will you?" she said nonchalantly, as he struggled amid a tangle of coats, scarves and the vacuum cleaner hose.

His face came up only inches from her own. "After I finish the kitchen, I might just look into organizing your closets," he said. "It's a wonder you find anything."

"Yes," she breathed, "it's really a wonder."

She knew him now, knew the crazy way he had of seeming to be always underfoot yet never in her way. She knew his penchant for sandwiches with lots of lettuce and the way he turned down his wool socks, just once, under his Levi's, above the tops of his hiking boots. She knew about his crazy curiosity, that might and often did lead in any direction. And she'd watched him with the children.

But most of all, she'd seen that look of deep hunger pass through his eyes like a winter storm, move off, leave him snowbound, unreachable. The fiercer the storm, the further he moved, and the more she knew she wanted to draw him close, touch him, warm him.

And she knew he was a flyer. Even now the suntanned, softly weathered face reminded her. Here today and gone tomorrow. She heard the memory of her childhood, felt the pain. But she wanted him. Whatever it would take. She felt her eyes widen with her own growing realization.

And she knew he saw it, written like a silent invitation on her face. "Adriana?" Her name fell off his tongue in a whisper that was half a question, half a groan. She could only stare at him, lips parted, speechless at her own realization.

His arms went around her, drawing her to himself, sheltering her against his chest. She marveled at the feel of them, the naturalness of the fit, remembering the first time he'd taken her hand in the woods . . . the butterfly woods, in autumn . . . butterfly autumn. Adriana hid her face and hugged him hard. From miles away, the phone rang and rang and rang.

"It will be Tony again," he whispered. "God, Adriana, what a time for your brother to suddenly decide he's ready to fly."

She had to force him to let her go. Tony? Ready to fly? She scrambled out of the closet and dashed for the phone. It was Felicia calling to say that Tony had already left. "He said to ask Scotty to meet him at the county airport. He said ten minutes."

Scotty lifted her in the air and swung her in a circle. Adriana hugged him tightly, heart pounding. "He'll make it," she said.

"He'd better," Scotty answered. "And when he does, I'll be back. Wait here. You will, won't you?"

"Yes," she said. Then petulantly, "No, I'm going skating."

"I'll find you," he called from halfway down the walk.

She watched him disappear, listening to the sound of the old Chevy pickup until the silence closed around her, until she almost heard the heavy rhythmic racing of her own heart.

She made herself move slowly. Straightening the closet, she rehung the fallen coats, replaced the broom, gathered the scattered contents of the box. There on the floor where they'd been sitting, both rabbit fur mittens snuggled side by side. She stared at them, an uncontrollable surge of hope mixed with trepidation washing over her. She caught up the mittens and her pink Annie Hall hat. Struggling into her gray parka, she dashed for the door. At the corner, she realized she'd forgotten her skates and had to go back for them.

"C'mon 'n' play!" the Bryant twins shouted from the center of the rink.

"I don't have a stick," she said, laughing. One boy shot the puck hard against the fence and Adriana cheered. If only she could burn off some of this...this *energy*. She sat down on the bench and laced her skates. Her fingers trembled. Snow fell, nestling gently into the laces. She thought of all the countless winters she'd done just this. Since childhood, skating had been her way of coping. Wrapping herself in silence, she would concentrate on glides, turns, jumps, until whatever it was that troubled her had melted like the ice beneath her flying blades.

The boys had finally had enough. They joined her on the bench. "It's all yours, Miss Anderson," they said good-naturedly.

Adriana stepped tentatively onto the ice. Round and round the small rink she moved, slowly at first, then with gathering speed. Her legs tired, then lightened, then tired again. She would not stop. If she stopped, she'd have to think. She couldn't think. *"I'll find you,"* he had said.

The fatigue passed, and she felt exhilaration take its place. She leaned into her crossovers, picking up speed. The snow swirled, scattering its own peculiar patterns around her. First snow, she thought. Second love? *No.* She'd never been in love with Calvin. Yet she'd been ready to marry him. How could she know if she loved Scotty now?

She tried the jump she'd learned last winter, fell, got up and tried again. By the fourth try she had it. The jump was smooth, controlled. With it she seemed to regain her own control. Her heart was beating from exertion not from some wild desire she dared not name. Scotty was her friend. Wasn't it best to keep it that way? She'd come so close to making a mistake with Calvin. Someone else would come along someday, someone who would fit the pattern.

"Scotty!" He'd been standing there a full five minutes, she learned, before she'd seen him. "How did it go?" She searched the tired lines of his face, the tense twitch to his left eye. She protested, but he insisted on unlacing her skates, massaging her tired feet in his strong, authoritative grasp.

"Tony's got guts. I've never seen anyone try so hard in all my life," he said. "Except for maybe you, when you tried that second jump."

"He'd do anything for Felicia," she said, shrugging off his compliment. "How did he do?"

"We didn't get off the ground," Scotty said. "But it doesn't matter. He sat in the cockpit for a good half hour. Then we taxied."

"Taxied?" Adriana repeated the word tentatively.

"I stopped after the first run," Scotty said. "He got out, stood at the edge of the runway and got sick."

"Oh, no," Adriana groaned.

"I told him to get the hell back in the plane or I'd leave him out there to freeze to death. I thought he was going to kill me. Then he got back in the cockpit, made me move over and taxied like the whole thing was just another milk run."

Adriana whooped for joy, jumped up off the bench and into Scotty's arms. "He did it!" she shouted. "He actually did it. He'll be flying in no time. I know it. Oh, Scotty, I love you!" The words had bubbled out, uncontrollably, she had no idea from where.

"You're so good," she added hastily. "You're the best friend I've ever had."

She almost wished she hadn't said it. The troubled look floated across his tired eyes, leaving them expressionless. Large, wet snowflakes fell between them on their clasped hands, making a miniature mound on her mittens. "Come on," she said. "I'll make us something for supper."

"I'll let you," he said hollowly, "provided it's edible." He slung her skates wearily over his shoulder. She took his arm and led him home.

Scotty stretched out on the old couch in the living room and kicked off his boots. He looked for all the world, she thought, like a hiker, an antique dealer, a general contractor—anything but the air force test pilot instructor that he was. She picked up his boots and set them by the fire to dry. Then she threw on another log.

His question surprised her. "Did you ever think of the Olympics?" he asked.

"Are you kidding?" she asked incredulously. "Why would I want to do that?"

"You're good," he said. "I used to watch the skating team train in Colorado Springs. You've got the grace, and the determination to be better. Maybe even the best."

"Umm," she answered, then watched him yawn and close his eyes. *To be the best.* That's what he wanted, wasn't it? And he'd go anywhere to prove it. I cannot love this man, she thought, dropping the afghan over him.

Adriana pulled a cushion from the chair, sat down before the fire and hugged her knees. Behind her, his slow rhythmic breathing told her Scotty slept deeply. She thought of the time he'd taken her to the air show and introduced her to the Blue Angels. Two of them had been his students. She had watched him tense when the planes had taken off, watched color fill his face and throb at his temples, felt his grip tighten on her elbow. He would never leave the air force. She'd known it then as she knew it now. But he would leave her. And it was likely to be soon. She curled herself around the cushion, wondering at the pain she felt at just the thought of losing him. If only there could be some way...

Biscuit stood on her chest, licking her nose to wake her up. Behind her, Scotty's sleep-washed eyes flickered in the firelight, his gaze caressing her hair, forehead, nose and chin. She remembered the day he'd lifted her sweater, aroused her with his worshipful touch. Adriana felt her face flush. She pushed Biscuit away and the small dog bounded over to Scotty, begging for attention.

"What were we talking about?" he asked, "before you fell asleep on me?"

"We were talking about how I promised you dinner," she fibbed, "before *you* fell asleep on *me*. Are you still interested?"

His gaze caught and held hers. Open, honest, not a trace of the storm. "'Interested' is a vast understatement." He lowered his voice to be sure she got the message.

"I'll just be a minute," she said, ignoring his tone. She warmed chicken noodle soup in the microwave, made coffee and toasted cheese sandwiches. They turned out golden brown, not burned as usual. Still, Scotty made a show of examining the food with care.

"Here, Biscuit!" He gave the dog a bite, pretending to wait for ill effects.

She bopped him soundly with the pot holder and ordered him to cut it out. He insisted on switching sandwiches with her, and then the soup. She drew the line at coffee. "I've already added cream," she reminded him. "You hate cream."

"So I do," he said, surprised, and reached for his sandwich. Beneath the table, his bare foot slid up her calf inside the leg of her jeans. She didn't pull away.

They ate in studied silence. What was he thinking? she wondered, her heart racing. What was *she* thinking? Calvin had never made her feel this way, not ever. On those surprisingly few weekends over the years at his house in Utica, Calvin's touch had left her empty, wondering what all the fuss was about. She'd hardly missed it when they'd stopped being intimate. And in the past year it was true—she had indeed deliberately avoided him. Yet Scotty had touched her once, and the memory of that night seemed burned into her body forever. Scotty, her friend, her dearest friend, could turn her body to liquid with just a touch.

When she rose to clear the table, he caught her wrist and pulled her down on his lap. "You were going to tell me something?'' he teased. "Don't keep me in suspense."

"Tell you something?"

"In the closet. It was written on your face. You lured me in there on purpose. Admit it."

"I did no such thing. I was looking for my mittens," she denied halfheartedly.

He traced the curve of her cheek with his hand. "I saw it here," he said. His hand moved to her eyes. She closed them as he caressed her lids. "And here," he breathed. And then his fingers traced the outer edges of her lips. "I'm sure I even saw it here."

His mouth covered hers in a long, deep kiss. She felt her body cup into his arms, cradle itself against his chest. In the hall beyond, the grandfather clock began a slow, sonorous chiming of the hour. The sound seemed to wrap her in a blanket of secure warmth. She drew him to herself.

"Tell me," he whispered. His breath on her cheek warmed through her, stirred her deepest needs, played some half-remembered symphony in her memory that ended in a dissonant chord.

What could she tell him? How could she put into words what she knew she felt? *I love you* carried so many unspoken promises. Ones she wasn't sure that she could keep. So much risk. She thought again of skating, imagined herself flying around the small rink, protected in a fantasy world of ice.

"I did have something to tell you," she began, skirting the issue. "Or rather, ask you."

"I'm all ears," he whispered, nuzzling her neck.

"I was just wondering if you'd thought anymore about staying around?"

"Staying around?" he asked. "As in for dessert? Or did you have something more daring in mind?"

"No," she said, feigning chagrin. "You know what I mean. Staying around here. The contracting job. Paradise Valley?"

The look that passed over Scotty's face turned Adriana's heart to stone and the words he spoke chiseled an epitaph. "I told you. I'm a flyer, Adriana. I'd be lousy at anything else."

"That's not true, Scotty," she blurted out. "You could do a thousand things. You're an incredible architect, a damn good chef, you have a mind that never stands still..." She was standing now, in the center of the kitchen. Her heart was saying what she had known since the moment she'd first set eyes on him. *Stay with me, Scotty. Please stay with me.* The words screamed in her brain. But when she spoke she could only say "Anything you tried you'd do well, Scotty. You're...creative. Whatever you touch, you leave your imprint."

He took hold of both her hands and rose as she spoke. She pulled her hands away; still she felt his touch. *You've left your imprint on me,* she thought.

"Don't pull away, Adriana," he said. "Hear me out." She stared into the brown-gold eyes, watched them calm, waited breathlessly for his answer.

"Don't you know by now? If those things are true, they're true *because* I'm a flyer. It's only by being what I am that I'm able to...to..." He was groping for the words. She wanted so to help him. And why couldn't she? There had to be a way.

"I...understand, Scotty. At least I think I do. It's a lot like how I feel about this house. Last winter when I couldn't write, when it seemed like graduate school and teaching and even Calvin's mother were smothering me, I came . . . home and it was all okay."

He seemed to be looking over her head, beyond her. She almost turned to look over her shoulder to try to see what he was looking at. Even his words seemed distant. "Home will always be important to you, Adriana. I hope you never lose your . . . hold on it."

She felt a sense of déjà vu. It was as though they were actors in a play, repeating lines they'd rehearsed months before, agreeing once again to simple friendship. Only this time they both understood the script. It wasn't just the U.S. Air Force for him or Calvin for her. He would move wherever flying took him because it was in his blood, and she would stay because she needed roots, permanence. Flying was in his soul, and her soul was in this house.

"Speaking of home," Scotty said, "it's late, I'm tired. I think I'll head for mine. Such as it is."

I want to come with you, Scotty, her heart whispered. Why couldn't she say it?

She walked him to the door, followed him onto the porch, reached to turn up the collar of his blue wool overcoat for him. Flakes of snow fell on the coppery strands turning them silver. She saw the hungry look in his eyes again.

He turned abruptly and started down the walk, took a few steps and floundered in the heavy snow. Beyond, the Sprite was nothing more than a drift of white. The winter season had dropped its first storm and it was, typically, a severe one. She heard him groan. "Have you got a snow shovel, Adriana?"

She brought two shovels, one for him and one for herself. When he protested, she simply threw him a dark look and pulled her Annie Hall hat farther down over her ears.

They worked for twenty minutes without speaking, shoveling vigorously until at last they'd cleared the walk. Leaning on their shovels, breathing hard, they turned to see another inch had fallen in their wake. Overhead, the streetlight was barely visible through the white sheet swirling below it. And nothing had passed on the street in front of them since they'd first begun to work.

"You'll never get the Sprite down the road," she said.

Scotty leaned on his snow shovel and peered into the blackness.

"This snow came earlier than they expected," she mused. "The plows aren't really ready. I don't think you're going anywhere, Mr. Scott." She'd tried to sound playful, light.

He turned to her then. The haunted look was back, filling his eyes with a desperate expression. *He was afraid.* She knew it now. He was desperately afraid of getting involved with her. She wasn't the only one with an entire style of life at risk. She looked back toward the street. The Sprite was totally invisible now. "I think you'd better plan to spend the night."

"I can't, Adriana." He nearly choked on the words.

Chapter Eight

Nonsense.'' It was Calvin's word. Now she was using it to deny the power of the force that attracted them. Adriana leaned the shovel against the porch rail. He had not followed.

''Come on,'' she said. ''You'll catch your death.'' She went on through the door, down the hall. Shaking the snow off her coat, she hung it on the hook inside the closet. Behind her, she heard the door open and close softly, heard Scotty's step in the hallway. Her heart raced.

She brushed nonchalantly by him, went directly to the study and pulled the cot out of the closet. ''Help me unfold this thing, will you?''

''You can have the whole downstairs to yourself,'' she said as they settled the cot back against the wall of the study. ''I'll bring you sheets and fresh towels for the shower off the laundry room.''

He still had not said a word; in fact, he still wore his coat, as though he really hadn't decided whether to stay. Her throat caught at the jaunty way his scarf hung, one side shorter than the other. She ached to straighten it. Instead she grasped the scarf in both her hands and looked directly into the light brown eyes.

"You could walk, Scotty," she said matter-of-factly. "Of course that would take about four hours in this mess." She saw his eyes flicker in amusement and pursued it. "Or the air base is about half an hour in the opposite direction. Maybe you could hitchhike!"

They listened intently; no cars had passed for at least an hour. The grin that spread across his face was broad and easy. Suddenly he was the friend she'd known all through the fall and into winter. She sighed with relief as he folded her gently in his arms, the wooly coat soft against her cheek.

"Just keep your distance, woman, and lock your door." The words brushed her ear so softly that she was hardly sure she'd heard them, thought instead she'd read his mind. She willed her heart to stop its erratic fluttering, groped through their mutual memories, searching for the warmth of friendship she'd learned to trust.

"I'll get the sheets," she said lightly. "Be back in a minute." She pulled away, moved up the stairs and quickly gathered the bed covers from the linen closet. On the landing, she paused and pulled aside the lace curtain. White flakes settled one by one into the latticework of the window. "It's still snowing hard," she said.

He stood at the foot of the stairs looking up at her. She felt her heart warm at the sight of him. Quickly she descended the stairs and filled his arms with the linen.

"Good night, Adriana," he said.

"Good night, Scotty." It came as a barely audible whisper. Automatically she raised her hand, brushed back a trailing lock of hair. She watched him set his jaw, turn, move off toward the study. Quickly she turned, too, and hurried back up the stairs.

Passing the linen closet, she grabbed a fresh towel and headed toward the bathroom. She filled the tub slowly with warm, steaming water, disrobed and sat naked at the dressing table. She brushed her long auburn hair over her full breasts. One hundred strokes forward, then one hundred strokes back. She brushed slowly, as though slowing the action could slow the rapid rate of her pulse. It was an old trick she'd used before her mother's parties when strangers whom she'd have to meet crowded the rooms downstairs. Now only one man waited downstairs, and he was anything but a stranger.

Waited? Adriana forced her thoughts away from the word, lingered instead on the small, comfortable things she'd learned about him, especially the incredible, absolutely insatiable curiosity. She remembered the time he'd picked a leaf off the windshield of the Sprite, the small brown bubble nest still attached.

"Oak-apple gall," she'd called it, and he'd made her explain every intricate detail of the worm that built the nest. "You're wrong," he'd said a week later. "*Britannica* says it's only on oak leaves."

Adriana caught a vision of herself in the dressing table mirror; the color in her cheeks was still high. Quickly she looked away. She piled her hair on top of her head with four large combs and tucked stray tendrils in with pins. She chose her favorite oil and added it to the bath, then trailed one hand through.

Sighing, she slipped into the silky hot cocoon and slid down almost to her hairline. The water flowed over her, relaxing every muscle till at last the roar of blood in her ears ceased. She lay motionless, listening to the quiet that enveloped the house. Her house. Forever.

She thought again of Scotty. He couldn't know she'd decided to break all ties with Calvin. Perhaps when she told him it would make a difference. Perhaps he was just waiting, wanting to be certain of her love. After all, one shouldn't take a career change lightly.

Adriana tensed as she heard the shower start directly below her. She closed her eyes, trying to shut out the images rising in her imagination. She'd forgotten to offer him shampoo. Could she towel off, slip into her robe, run it down to him? *No.*

Behind her closed eyes the images persisted. She imagined his own mink-colored eyes closed against the pounding water as it threaded through the copper-blond hair, ran down the rugged face, the corded neck, lingered in the mat of curling coppery hairs that covered his chest.

Her imaginary gaze insisted on continuing downward, over the taut muscles of his abdomen, down the thin trail of curling hair that led to the rich, ripe swell of his manhood. Adriana felt as though all the furtive glances she'd hardly been aware she'd been taking had united to tantalize her, unnerve her with their throbbing intensity.

She reached for her bath mitt and began to lather herself slowly. She turned on the hot water, letting it seep into the tub, focusing on the sound of the steady stream, letting it drown out the sound of the shower below. But nothing seemed to calm the incessant flutter in the space below her navel, nor smooth the stiff, hard peaks of her swelling breasts.

Finally Adriana climbed out onto the bath rug and toweled herself off. She could not help thinking of that day when she had hardly known him, the wonderful release she'd felt when he'd undone her bra, worshiped the smooth, olive-colored swell of her breasts, tantalized the dark, erect tips. That day had been a discovery, one that she'd tried to deny ever since. Now as she toweled herself in the steam-filled bathroom, she faced the naked desire that had crept into his eyes so often.

She pulled on her camel-colored robe, slipped into fleece-lined slippers, turned out the light and glided across the hall to her bedroom. Not bothering to turn on a light, she closed the door. No lock. She'd never noticed. She crossed the room and huddled in the bay window seat. Outside, the snow fell steadily.

She hugged her knees and shivered. Beyond, the roof of the porch lay covered in snow. Eight inches at least, she guessed. Below her, she heard the unmistakable sound of pacing. It stopped, started again, stopped. Perhaps he stood in the living room bay window as she sat in this one. What could he be thinking? *"Just keep your distance, woman."* The words echoed in her head as his footsteps began again.

Adriana pressed her face against her knees. She'd never been lonely in her house before. Now she was hardly alone, yet loneliness seemed to blanket the house within, as the heavy snow blanketed it outside.

The pacing had started again, and with each step her heart echoed, hollow and empty.

Adriana got up and opened her closet, shivering in the cold as she took off her robe and slipped into her gown. She settled herself between the icy sheets of her brass bed, and stared at the ceiling.

Outside, the waving branches of the pine made soothing noises, and gathered the streetlight's glow to cast dim, lacy patterns on the ceiling of her room. The pacing had stopped. She lay, listening to the silence. Far away she thought she heard the distant drone of the plows.

Would he dress and leave once they'd cleared the street? Would she wake to an empty house, to one of the funny notes she used to find stuck on the fridge when she'd returned from a date with Calvin? Calvin. *"You're wasting your life,"* he'd said. And she knew it was true, not an intellectual sort of knowing but a gut-level, wrenching feeling. For weeks she'd been using Calvin to hide from . . . something . . . from Scotty? Why?

The tea kettle's shrill whistle penetrated the silence. Adriana started. It stopped immediately, then she heard the scrape of a kitchen chair, the click of the cabinet door. He hadn't gotten around to fixing the hinge. Maybe there wouldn't be time . . .

In her mind, she saw him reach for the tea. The canister was nearly empty. He wouldn't know where to find the extra tea bags, she thought, tossing off the covers. *No,* she thought the moment her feet touched the cold bedroom floor.

She stood there shivering in the chilly bedroom, poised between the bed and the closed door. The gentle slam of the study door startled her.

Biscuit. Had she fed him? Of course. He'd be yelping his head off by now if she hadn't. And the front door—had she locked it? She shrugged. What did it matter since Scotty slept only inches from it. Had she given him enough blankets? Adriana wrapped her own arms around herself, felt her icy fingers through the thin gown.

She turned then and stood in front of the tall, oval cheval mirror. In the streetlight from the window opposite she stared at her image. Why was she searching for excuses? Slowly she reached to the hair still piled atop her head. One by one she pulled out the pins and then the combs until her heavy auburn hair fell in waves over her shoulders.

The warmth started somewhere near her heart and spread throughout her body until she had to moisten her lips to keep them from parching. Barefoot, she crossed the room, opened the door and moved softly down the stairs.

Light filtered under the door of the study. She knocked softly, then pushed it open. He sat, propped against a pillow in the corner, naked to the waist. One jean-clad leg bent, he balanced the cup of hot tea on his knee. In the dim light of her study lamp, she thought she saw a glisten on one cheek, perhaps moisture from the shower, or steam from the cup.

Adriana crossed the room, slowly, hesitantly. He set the cup on a nearby windowsill and stood. The bulk of his body seemed to fill the room as he reached out to her. The strong cords pulsed in his neck. The hard, heavily muscled arms wrapped firmly around her. She buried her face in the clean furry warmth of his chest and shuddered as the arms closed tightly around her, pulling her thighs against his own. She felt like hot lead pressed into its mold. The single teardrop stung as it hit her cheek.

She looked up quickly to see the wet track of the tear across his firm, tanned cheek. The golden flecks swam in his earth-toned brown eyes. Adriana felt a choking rise to her throat. Had she hurt him by coming to him or by staying away so long? Was it the past he wept for? Or was it the darkness of the future?

She had no time to ask, for his mouth came down on hers with a force that nearly made her fall. She clutched at the back of his neck, half to keep herself from falling, half to draw him closer.

She felt his mouth melt into hers, draw in her restless tongue, taste it, caress it, tease it with his own. He found her ear and nipped it, then thrust his tongue into its tiny opening. Adriana shuddered with delight.

But it was his hands that turned her to liquid—warm, caressing, as they traveled over her body. He touched the small of her back, traced the curve of her spine, explored the swell of her hips. His hand slid under the hem of her short nightgown, and he groaned with the pleasure at what he found.

She stood away from him then, eyes lowered, trembling. He turned off the light. She took his hand in her own and moved toward the open door.

At the foot of the stairs he swept her up, carried her up them, past the landing where the snow fell thick and fast against the window beyond the lace curtain. He paused there to kiss her, his breath and hers frosting the diamond-shaped panes of glass.

He tucked her head against his chest and carried her the rest of the way upstairs, set her down in the half-lit room beside the brass bed. Slowly, carefully, he lifted the gown, then dropped it in a gauzy heap at the foot of the bed.

She stood before him naked, proud and unashamed. Unconscious of the chilliness of the room, she felt her blood race through her veins, warming her before the golden flicker of his worshipful eyes. He cupped her face, pushed back the auburn hair from both her temples, kissed her there. Everywhere. The soft wafts of kisses fell on her memory, recalling the butterfly meadow. Adriana longed to press the fluttering jeweled insects against her naked skin, longed to hold Scotty still.

He lifted her, placed her gently in the bed. She opened her eyes, looked up to the man who stood over her. His chest rose and fell heavily as he struggled to control his breath. His face wore the look of naked hunger she'd seen him try to hide so often. Now it was as though everything he'd suppressed had risen to the surface. The look frightened her. Only the gold-brown eyes kept her from crying out.

His hands went to his waist. Strong, slightly callused—she knew them well. She watched him loosen his belt, step out of his trousers, turn to toss them aside. He wore nothing underneath. In the half light of the streetlamp she traced the smooth, sensual curve of his lower back and the granite, muscular curve of his naked buttocks. "Scotty?" she whispered.

"Here, love." He turned and she saw the full glory of the rising swell of his manhood. He stretched himself out on the bed beside her and pulled her body to himself.

She kissed him then. Starting with his mouth, she bent over him, her long hair covering their kiss like boughs of pines in a dark secluded forest. She kissed his neck below his ear where his pulse throbbed strong and hard, and she tasted the hollow of his neck below the prominent collarbone. She kissed the inside of his elbow inhaling the fresh, clean scent of him. Her fingers tangled in the mass of hair at his chest, and she withdrew them to tease and stroke his hardened nipples with her persistent tongue.

He grasped her arms to hold her back but Adriana felt fire course through her veins, and with it a power that insisted on having its way. And he did not resist but held her head, pressed it gently as she explored the tense muscles of his lower belly.

His body tensed, went rigid as he struggled to endure her intimate kiss. Adriana heard his groan, rising like thunder before the rain, but she fought to hold him longer, kiss him more deeply.

He lifted her then and moved her gently to the pillow by his side, smoothed her arms, her legs, her torso into the bed. In the power of his touch, she realized that her own strength had been illusory. He'd only let her have her way. Now he would claim his own.

She closed her eyes as he bent over her. Now his kisses were more insistent. Her lips swelled under the pressure of his mouth, opened to the demands of his tongue. She felt his teeth against her own. His tongue laid siege to her mouth, probing its inner recesses till every hidden spot had been explored.

Only then did he move his mouth away, allowing her to breathe. "Scotty..." she stammered. "Scotty...I..."

"Shh, love," he whispered. "I want to take my time."

She tried to quiet the throbbing in her belly, tried to still the deafening roar of her own blood pounding against her temples, beating against her eardrums. He kissed first one breast, then the other, circling the tingling nipples with his tongue, his mouth taking small, teasing bites. Adriana cried out in pleasure and desire.

She lost all sense of time, space, motion. Thought of nothing except the feel of his touch and the way he moved against her. Wherever he touched her she arched into him until the subtlest pressure from his mouth was guiding her in the direction he chose.

Then he was covering her body with his own, his legs exerting gentle but persistent pressure against her thighs until she lay open, vulnerable, ready for his thrust. He moved, and time, the room, the world, moved with him, sliding into her femininity. She met his heat with her own and together they burst into a world she'd never known existed until now.

She held on tightly as the tense hardness of his throbbing manhood matched itself against the rhythmic pulsing of her body's love. She won the race, arched her body, lifting his, crying out with the ecstasy of it. He came close behind her, groaning into the pillow, his breath hot and ragged as it swept across her breast. He grasped her hips and thrust one final time, adding his ecstasy to her own.

Waves upon waves of it washed over them both, cleansed them of all their living up till now. Then Adriana knew. He'd wept not for past or future but for the moment. The moment that was now. She closed her eyes and slept against him.

Somewhere in the night they found each other again. Loved quieter, deeper, fuller. And then they slept again. Adriana dreamed of the mountains in Colorado where the snow falls deep and never melts.

Adriana woke, stretched, covered her eyes against the blinding sunlight as it bounced off the thick blanket of snow coating the porch roof and illuminating the entire room with its brilliance. She rolled into the warmth left by Scotty's body, buried her face in his pillow, breathed deeply the musky smell of lovemaking that lingered in the rumpled bed.

She heard the familiar noise of the perking coffeepot, the clank of the cast-iron skillet as he pulled it from the oven and set it on the stove. Adriana opened her eyes. The butterfly sheet seemed to come alive. The tiny insects danced in the dappled light as it bounced off the mirror opposite the window and fell upon the bed.

She moved her fingers among the forms, recalling other moments, other memories. She felt his hair in her hands, the hard press of her body against his. Adriana felt a song rise in her throat. Some half remembered melody, or was it one she'd never heard? She reached for words to match the melody ringing in her ears. Then she knew. She knew it as surely as she knew her own name. "I love him," she whispered aloud to the butterflies brought to life by the sunlit morning. "I love him!"

Adriana swung out of bed, pulled on just her robe and stepped into her slippers. She flew down the stairs and caught him just as he turned from the sink. He stood there, arms folded across his bare chest, his shining eyes inquisitive.

And suddenly she felt shy with her message. He came to her, gathered her in his arms.

"I love you, Adriana," he said, his voice low and mellow, merging into her own "I love you, Scotty."

They stood, savoring the moment, like long-time lovers who've forgotten there ever was a life apart.

Then they took their coffee cups to the window seat in the dining room and sat, watching the field outside as it glistened gemlike in the warming sun.

"The plows never made it this far," she said, surveying the street beyond.

"The radio said the schools are all closed, including U.C. The phone's dead, but I'm not due at the base until midnight, anyway."

"Then we have the day!" she said excitedly.

"Yes." He smiled into her eyes. "We have the day." An elusive shadow crept into the corners of his eyes. She'd have to ask him. They'd have to talk. Was there any possibility their separate dreams could mesh, merge into one? Whatever it was, she would not face it now, not in this incredible, closed-off world where only he and she existed, where only the moment mattered.

He brought her eggs, scrambled with bits of cheese and jalapeño pepper. And she filled his cup and hers again, and they sat at opposite ends of the sunbeam that stretched across the long dining room table and relished breakfast.

Both of them fed Biscuit under the table. They'd given up long ago resisting the puppy's pleas.

Adriana gathered and stacked the breakfast things while Scotty showered. Then she remembered, ran upstairs for shampoo and handed it to him through the shower curtain. He grabbed her wrist and refused to release it, and so she slipped out of her robe and squeezed into the tiny shower stall with him.

She scrubbed his back and he scrubbed hers, and the washing turned into caressing and hungry loving and union as the warm water poured over them both.

Wrapped again in her robe, Adriana lay on the bed, her long hair draped over the side as he brushed and dried it for her. She felt his fingers slide into her hair, massage her scalp, trail down, gently pulling the tangles loose. Then his hand strayed to the deep, loose V of her robe. Parting it, he began caressing the exposed curves of her breasts.

She felt the desire rise in her and she pulled him down on top of her.

"Lie on me, Scotty," she begged. "Cover me." She felt his skin make contact with her own—mouth on mouth, fingertip to fingertip. They moved together like underwater dancers, like paired figure skaters, like butterflies mating in flight. The rise and fall of her hips met the rhythmic thrust of his groin, captured, clasped, drained it dry.

At last he rolled to his side, pulling her with him, holding her fast. The laughter started in them both at nearly the same moment. Hers was waves of uncontainable happiness; his was deeper, undulating currents covering her laughter with his own much as he had covered her body.

"Come on," she said, "I've got a surprise for you." They dressed each other, laughing at the awkwardness of it. She pulled his shorts on backward and he could not seem to clasp her bra without pinching her unmercifully. She laced his boots and he laced hers. Finally ready, she pulled him out the side door toward the garage. In knee-deep snow they trudged, floundered, fell laughing over each other. At last they reached the garage, cleared the snowbound side door and stepped inside.

He had to help her lift the toboggan. It was very old, made of seasoned hickory wood, the rim worn smooth where she and Tony and their parents had ridden, time and again, whenever they had shared a snowy winter. In the dim light of the garage, Adriana almost heard the laughter of her childhood. She paused, her throat closing on the memory. There had been no snow in Turkey. She had agreed to keep the toboggan.

"There's a hill behind the grade school down the block." She said the words more to herself than to him, testing the timbre of her voice. It did not tremble. Gratefully she picked up her end of the toboggan and followed him out the door.

By the time they reached Linden Street, the first plow was moving down its center, cutting a wide swath of snow-packed roadway bordered by heaps of shoveled snow. They paused for a moment, watching the plow disappear. It would not be long, Adriana knew, before the plows would have the city cleared. Then they'd have to go their separate ways.

Suddenly, with a rowdy war whoop, Scotty cleared the snow heaps in a single leap and took off down the street. She had to run with him to keep from dropping her end of the toboggan. He didn't stop until he'd reached the top of the hill, settled her in front of him and bribed some kids into pushing them off.

Then wind, trees, snowsuited children flashed by as they sped down the hill, bumped once, twice, flying into the air and landing hard with every loop. It was one wild, unchosen, heady risk of a ride and Adriana loved it.

They sped down the hill, then trudged to its top and sped down again, each time adding more and more children until Adriana was certain that the old toboggan would sink into the snow and fail to budge. But the warm sun had melted the top layer and the cold air had turned it to a crust of crisp ice, and time and again the limber sled sped down the hill, spilling its laughing cargo of children at the bottom.

"I thought you didn't like kids," he said.

"Oh, no," she said, laughing. "It was Calvin. He said they made him nervous." Adriana hugged a tiny red-haired girl, then passed her back to her mother. When she turned to Scotty, she was surprised to see a pained look had clouded his eyes. "Scotty, it's over between Calvin and me. It's been over for some time." She knew instantly she'd misinterpreted the look.

"I know that, Adriana," he said quietly, but the look lingered as Scotty gathered up loose mittens and knocked the packed snow off the toboggan. Adriana knew that it was time to ask the first of her innumerable questions, time to risk breaking the silence. She searched for words. As they reached her house and mounted the steps to the front porch, the heavy plows continued to clear James Street.

"I'll do the walks," he said casually. "It's the least I can do to thank you for your hospitality." His voice was strangely wooden, as though he'd left part of himself on the toboggan hill and only brought his shadow back.

"Hospitality?" Adriana tasted the word then spat it back to him. "Hospitality! Is that what you call what we've shared?"

He grabbed her roughly, tipped her chin and kissed her hard. "Of course not," he said, then added an expletive.

"I love you, Scotty. I'm sorry it took me so long to know it. And you love me. There's got to be a way to work things out." The words tumbled out, racing over one another. "I guess I never loved Calvin at all," she said. "I...I think I used him. After my parents' death I was trying to discover who I was. He was somehow a part of it."

"Perhaps it was the other way around." Scotty's voice still sounded hollow. "Perhaps he used you. Don't ever let anyone try to tell you who you are, Adriana. Calvin tried to do that by denying you children."

"He took me in, or at least his mother did," she persisted. "I had insisted on using my inheritance to pay off this house."

"You're really attached to it, aren't you?" She felt his hand tremble as he pressed her hard to his chest.

"It's as though I know every inch of it. As though I've left a part of myself on every wall. Don't you feel the same about your houses, Scotty?"

"I love the houses while I'm building them," he said gently. Adriana felt weak, as though he was about to break some difficult news to her. "But I know I have to let them go, so I hold back a little."

"My mother was like that," Adriana said quietly. "She'd sell nearly everything and start fresh, as though she knew she'd one day lose it all, and therefore wanted there to be less to part with."

"I've been like that," Scotty said, "until now." He tipped her head and she looked into his brown-gold eyes. The laughter had returned and she smiled into it.

"It's that damn kitchen, Adriana," he teased. "I couldn't hold back this time. This, you, are home to me now."

"Oh, Scotty," she cried, "then you'll stay? Leave the air force? Go with the project?"

The look that passed over his face turned her heart to ice. She felt it put miles between them as surely as his going away. "It's not that easy, Adriana," he said. "I...I've gotten papers..." he ran his hand nervously through his hair. She wanted to grab his wrist and keep him from doing it.

"Women...need a nest. I fly."

"But you need a nest, too!" she said. "Why can't it be here?"

"I...I do need a home Adriana. I need *you*." He pulled her closer, held her fiercely. "I wish I could ask you to fly with me, Adriana." The liquid sweetness of the words smoothed the rough edges of his husky voice. She thought of the butterflies, the ones who wouldn't make the migratory journey. She thought of them heaped against her windshield, wings beating in one last frantic effort. His breath came in soft, tentative whispers. "Houses can be built anywhere, Adriana, even in California."

"California! You've got to be kidding. It's not just the house I want Scotty, it's...it's community, small town, permanence, history, everything that California *isn't*."

He held her at arm's length then. She watched the warmth in his eyes withdraw as though to some far off memory. "Perhaps Calvin, or someone like him, can give you that, Adriana," he said quietly. "But if he does, you'll wish to God he hadn't."

She tried to hit him, her small tight fists pounding the chest she'd fondled only hours ago. He caught her wrists and she threw back her hair in a violent sweep. "Why did you love me like that, Scotty, knowing you'd be leaving..."

"Why the hell did you come down those stairs, Adriana? I never said I'd stay."

Chapter Nine

Adriana stood alone in the empty hallway. The echo of the slammed door passed her once, then seemed to fill the house through and through. Anger and sorrow rose in her throat, and she swallowed them both. She wandered from room to room touching, remembering.

But he loved her. He'd made it so abundantly, so beautifully, so sensually clear. Her house, he'd said, was home to him. Yet he was going away. *How soon?* If only he could wait till she was ready. If she'd *ever* be ready.

In the dining room window seat, Adriana pulled her knees to her chin and hugged them tightly. Outside, the snow melted steadily under the warm sun of early afternoon. The children's snowman had already lost his head and ugly muddy puddles were forming in the trampled field. Above, Adriana noticed that the stained glass border of the window needed washing.

She looked away, to the table, then found her vision filled with her and Scotty's coffee cups, empty but for the dregs of the morning.

Adriana set her chin defiantly, gathered up the cups and carried them to the kitchen, setting them none too gently on the cocoa-colored ceramic tile counter. They'd argued about the color. She'd liked dark brown, but he'd reminded her that a lighter shade would catch and reflect the scant sunlight from the room's single window. He had been right, of course. She traced the single golden streak that cut through the pane, hit the counter, bounced off the butterfly magnets fastened to the refrigerator.

Scotty had found the magnets and had used them to leave her little notes. She'd find them after work or, more often, after being out with Calvin. "Lock up" or "Extra spaghetti in fridge" or "Biscuit's getting fat." He'd waited for her all this time. Surely he wouldn't give up now.

Tuesday morning, Adriana rose early, half from wakefulness, half to get an early start on the roads. There wasn't any need. The plows had done a thorough job the night before. She headed toward the college, the sun rising in the grayness before her.

She moved mechanically through the day. Yesterday's forced holiday had made the students even more eager for Thanksgiving break and discussion was disjointed. Calvin insisted on lunch. Reluctantly she agreed to meet him at the usual time.

"You look like you need a vacation," he said, between bites of Swiss steak drenched in gravy. Adriana watched a small trickle of gray liquid work its way down Calvin's chin. Instinctively she reached out with her napkin to wipe it away. He caught her hand and held it.

"Adriana," he began, his voice low and throaty, "I've missed you so."

She watched the tremble in his chin begin. How could she tell him now? And what was there to tell? *I'm in love with another man, Calvin,* she'd rehearsed, *it's the real thing. Not gratitude. Not a search for security. Love. Of course, he's going away... probably for good...and he agrees I need to stay here.* It sounded ridiculous, even as she thought it.

"You'll be back by Sunday noon?" Calvin reminded her. "It's Mother's birthday, you know, and she's expecting us."

"Of course," she said vaguely, "unless we have another storm."

"Tony's friend is almost finished with your kitchen, right? You won't be seeing him anymore?"

It was the first mention Calvin had made of Scotty in two months and the first indication that he saw Haines Scott as a threat. Perhaps he'd guessed that her feelings for Scotty hadn't been clear until that moment.

"He's been reassigned to Edwards—"

"Yes, I remember," Calvin interrupted. "He said he'd been expecting orders at the dinner over Labor Day. Lucky he finished your kitchen first."

Adriana felt the room begin to spin. She shut her eyes tightly, trying to steady her whirling mind. *Scotty had known all along he'd be going so soon and still he'd kept after her.* She'd told him she'd never move. What was it then—a game? She thought of Tony's warning. And he'd gotten to her through her house. Now every time she looked in that kitchen, or slept on that bed, she'd think of him. Not satisfied with just her body, he'd made himself a part of everything she loved.

Anger welled in Adriana and overflowed. She'd tell Calvin everything. He'd be angry. He'd find Scotty and...and... "I didn't know you were jealous of Scotty," she blurted out.

Calvin stopped chewing midbite and stared at her. "Jealous?" he mumbled. She knew in that moment that the notion had never crossed his mind. "It's just that, well, Professor Howard who lives across the street from you is always remarking about how often that decrepit red truck or the Sprite is parked in front of your house...and...you *do* know how I hate gossip."

She stiffened. Of course. Calvin always worried about what people thought. She'd forgotten about Howard. It was one of those things she liked least about small-town life. Howard would probably tell Calvin about Sunday night. The Sprite had spent the night in front of her house. Calvin did not deserve to find out that way.

"Calvin..." she began again, but he had already risen, pulled out his pocket watch and begun gathering up papers.

"It's five after one, Adriana. You're late."

"It's only five after one because you set your watch eight minutes fast," she reminded him, knowing it was useless to argue. Calvin was always trying to hurry her up.

"So?" he said. "You'd better dash. I have a meeting all day tomorrow, so I can't see you off. And you have your class at the base tonight. Call me Sunday afternoon when you get back. And check your tires before you take off," he called as he rushed off. "You know you get better mileage if you've got evenly balanced tires."

Calvin was an authority on good mileage. In fact, he'd been initially impressed by her savvy in choosing the VW. She'd never bothered to tell him that she'd bought it because a friend of Tony's had needed the money. She sat for a moment watching Calvin's back disappear into a crowd of students, then gathered up her own papers and tried to be brisk.

At odd moments all afternoon, Adriana rehearsed her greeting. Still, at 7:00 p.m. as she drove through Skyline gate, she was no more ready to face Scotty than she'd been last night, alone in the empty hallway at home after he'd left. But by 7:15 and then by 7:30, Scotty's chair was still empty. She worried till one of the other students asked for an extra assignment sheet. No explanation, just "Major Scott said to tell you he's sorry."

Sorry? Sorry for what? Sorry he'd met her? Sorry he'd carried it so far? If he was sorry, she could be sorrier.

She told him as much later that night when he finally called. The conversation began as countless others had begun. Only the tone was different, strained and hesitant.

"I'll be over Thursday to work on the kitchen."

"I won't be here."

"I've got my key."

"Will you feed Biscuit?"

"Don't I always?"

She listened to the hollowness in his voice. In a matter of days, he'd be the one who wouldn't be here. She'd be the one to feed Biscuit. He'd give her back the key to the side door. She could almost feel the cold metal against her palm. "You're almost finished with the kitchen, aren't you?" She felt her voice trail off as if adjusting to the distance already.

"Adriana . . . Adriana, don't do this to us." He'd groaned out the words.

She listened for more. Silence. "Do what?" she floundered. "I don't see that anything I do matters. And anyway, you knew you'd be leaving. You knew it from the beginning. Why did you . . ."

"Why did I do *what*?" he demanded. "I did my damnedest to give you room. You were the one who came down those stairs. You *chose*, Adriana. You can't deny me that."

His words plummeted into her heart like lead dropped into the icy water of a shot tower. They shaped themselves cylindrically, hard, like indestructible tears that promised to weight her down forever. So he hadn't really wanted her. It came to her now. Tony's warning, Scotty's own "I'll never marry." She'd left herself wide open. The phone slid from her hand. Adriana picked it up and placed it back in its cradle.

The phone rang again instantly and four more times that evening. Adriana ignored it. She sat in the study and worked till midnight. Then typed the last of her stories. She'd proof it when she returned. The M.A. would be granted on schedule. With any luck, she'd save enough next month for a rug. The floor grew colder by the day and the echoes of the clock, striking its way through the hours, were more than she could stand.

Finally Adriana curled into a corner of the big brass bed with Biscuit at her feet. Before she slept, she planned how she would rise early, pack and leave for D.C. immediately following her one o'clock class, and thus eliminate all possibility of facing Scotty.

Adriana stared in disbelief at the tiny figure whose face was framed in the lamplit, oval glass of the Georgetown doorway. She felt as though a mirror image smiled back at her. The auburn hair, piled elegantly on top of Aunt Beatrice's head, contrasted only with the looseness of her own. The wide-set brown eyes above the same high, Mediterranean cheekbones, still clear and sensitive at fifty-six matched her own. Only the tired smile lines, which testified to the fact that Beatrice's life had demanded the smile rather than given it, were absent from her own face. Even the unhurried way her aunt opened the door and led her into the living room reminded Adriana of herself.

"Are you all right, my dear?" A cool cheek was pressed to her own and Adriana heard a quiet, unpretentious voice tinged with unspoken regret, but lacking the bitterness she'd expected.

"I'm sorry," she said. "Tony told me I looked a lot like you, but I had no idea..."

"I'm sorry, too," her aunt said distantly, "for all the years we could have shared. When I last saw you, you hardly said a word. Dressed in your Sunday best, you sat in this very room and listened. Your mother, bless her, rattled on and on about the move to Japan and how they'd need next to no furniture. Did you really sleep on the floor?"

"I can't remember," Adriana said with a laugh. "I was so young, and I think the Japan tour was one of the shorter ones. All I remember was wishing I could stay here in D.C. with you." She looked around the living room as she spoke and felt a distant familiarity settle down around her.

"Well . . . yes . . . of course you were too young to realize . . ." The older woman lowered her eyes and traced the lace of a lavender-colored handkerchief, her slender fingers smoothing it on her lap repeatedly. "This was no place for a child in those days—ever in fact. But I'm glad you're here now." She added the last part briskly, then moved through the elegant dining room and on to the kitchen.

Adriana stopped to admire the heavy oak dining table, still lustrous despite its age. "You'll take that, of course," Aunt Beatrice remarked. "I would so hate to see it go out of the family."

Adriana tried to imagine the beautiful table in her dining room at home. Instead she kept seeing Scotty, seated at her own secondhand table, holding his coffee mug the way he always did, by the upper rim . . .

"This is Nedra," Aunt Beatrice introduced the diminutive maid. "My niece will be dining with us over the holidays, Nedra, so we'll cook the small turkey, after all." The woman nodded politely.

"I wasn't sure you'd make it with the storm last week," Beatrice went on. "Nedra's new. I haven't had a maid since Robert . . . got ill," her aunt explained, voice faltering.

"I'm sorry about Uncle Robert's death," Adriana responded quickly.

"Don't be," her aunt answered cryptically. "He brought it on himself, with the aid of alcohol, of course."

Following the graceful figure up the stairs, Adriana could almost imagine herself, twenty years down the road. Had she married him, Calvin might have left her widowed early. She paused on the landing and looked out the window. The dark, unwelcoming windows in the brownstone across the way reminded her of Calvin's house in Utica.

"I've made up the extra bedroom for you, Adriana," Aunt Beatrice interrupted her thoughts. "Your mother slept there when she was growing up."

The bed was cherrywood and canopied in white eyelet. Adriana ran her palm down the smooth post. It was nothing like her mother, she thought, yet it recalled a part of her that Adriana half remembered. The dainty matching bureau was polished to a shine, as was the small desk. A child's rocker stood in one corner, its cane seat in disrepair.

"I've just learned caning in a class!" Adriana exclaimed. "I could redo this." She stopped to count the empty holes in the chair's seat. Her tears flowed freely then. For her mother and for all she'd left behind and for her own loss. This room remained—only it was still unchanged. And somehow Adriana knew and understood. Nothing could ever replace this room. Why try? So her mother had left it and moved on, had bought new furniture, tried new things. If she'd reached Turkey she'd have ridden camels and hung her walls with brass plates. Adriana wept for the future her mother had lost, not the past.

Beatrice bent, creases of concern deepening the smile lines around her mouth. "I'm sorry dear, perhaps you'd prefer to sleep elsewhere. There's a daybed in the sewing room. I thought after six years . . ."

"Oh, no." Adriana clung to the older woman. "I'm all right. I'd love to sleep here. It's just that I finally understood something about mother."

"Then you've come further in a moment than I have in years," the older woman responded.

"You have her eyes. We both do," Adriana said later over a late-night cup of tea.

"I'm afraid that's all I have," Aunt Beatrice responded. "Your mother had an aloof quality, bravado and insatiable curiosity."

Like Scotty, Adriana thought. "She always said you thought she was 'flighty.'" Adriana mused aloud. "She used to flit around when she said it, as though proving your point. I tended secretly to agree with you."

"She was like that from the beginning," Beatrice said. "She was six years old the day we landed in New York City. I lost her in the airport, and when she turned up an hour later in the arms of an army sergeant, she'd learned half a dozen words in English including 'chocolate ice cream.' Of course she answered that she'd been 'nowhere.' I should have known then that she'd end up marrying someone in uniform, someone she'd fallen in love with, totally beyond reason. I did everything I could to see that she'd have security, a proper home..."

Adriana kept silent. She'd heard the story many times. "Poor Beatrice," her mother would sigh. "I've worried her so. She can't forget how hungry we all were the year we lost Papa." When they'd finally made it to the States, Beatrice had "married well" and stayed behind and her sister had set off with Capt. Adrian Anderson to see the world. "Like a butterfly," Adriana mused aloud.

"Like what?" Beatrice set her demitasse in the saucer carefully.

"I was just thinking," Adriana said, "that my mother was like a butterfly."

"Hm..." Beatrice mused. "How true that is. I wonder that I'd never thought of it. Perhaps you'd like to see your mother's collection?"

"Collection?" Adriana asked.

"We'll start in the attic tomorrow," Beatrice promised. "We're both too weary to begin tonight."

Too tired to dream, Adriana fell instantly asleep as soon as she got into bed.

"I have no idea what you'll want to keep or take for Tony," Beatrice said the next morning as they climbed the stairs to the attic. "We'll just make a list and have it sent. You won't hurt my feelings one bit by turning anything down."

"You're getting rid of everything?" Adriana asked, puzzled. "I don't understand. You've spent a lifetime collecting. Every room is filled with beautiful antiques. You've had them forever. You have... roots."

Her aunt turned slowly at the landing. "I only hope they won't be impossible to pull up, Adriana. Roots are like that—they hold you back sometimes, when you'd best be moving on."

"But they also hold you up," Adriana countered. "They remind you who you are."

"Were," her aunt insisted.

"I beg your pardon?"

"Roots remind you of who you were, where you come from. Today you are someone new, different, alive and growing."

They'd reached the attic by then, and Adriana gasped in delight at the cluttered array.

She thought of her own attic, wondering how many years it would take to build up the wonderful profusion of items. There were articles temporarily out of use, luggage, old trunks. There were items still useful, but just needing to be mended, like the maple chair missing one rocker. Then there were inherited treasures, gifts from her mother like the Oriental fan, a scroll, a silver hair ornament. Among these were an array of white elephants that would never be used, and discarded household items. All of it was far too dear ever to be thrown away.

Adriana followed her aunt to a folding table set up under a dusty floor lamp. She watched, fascinated, as Beatrice rummaged through countless boxes marked Collections. One entire box brimmed with seashells. They spent at least an hour fingering them. Aunt Beatrice could identify none of the shells precisely. She could only offer vague memories of leisurely days at this beach or that.

"I gathered shells while Robert drank," she said. "He always said the sound of the the waves made him thirsty." She laughed in a fragile, high-pitched soprano that made Adriana wince and recall her mother's word for Beatrice—"tragic."

At last Beatrice spread the small glass cases on the table before them. Butterflies of every size and description, mounted on white cotton, spread their wings to reveal still vibrant hues of gold, metallic blues and greens. They were as exquisite as jewels and Adriana caught her breath.

"I planted a butterfly tree off the back veranda," Beatrice explained, "the Jewel Tree shrub attracted all of them. We used to send unusual specimens to the Smithsonian for identification. They'd write and tell us all sorts of interesting facts." Beatrice pointed proudly to the small typed labels, frowned at a yellowed one and plucked at it nervously.

Adriana touched the cold glass of the display cases. Beneath it the butterflies hung motionless, their colors brilliantly preserved for all time. She stared from them to Beatrice, her hair still auburn, her eyes still rich, bright brown. Adriana saw herself. Was that all there was to living, then—preserving things, memories, even people? No, she thought, and her mother, too, had known otherwise.

"I'm...I'm awfully tired," Adriana said suddenly. "Perhaps we could rest for a while."

"I'm sorry, dear. Of course—how thoughtless of me."

Adriana crawled again between the cool sheets, breathed deeply of the room that smelled of lavender and old furniture polish. Perhaps she'd fill her house with a mixture—some new things, not everything antique. And she might plant a butterfly tree. But she knew she didn't want the collections. Adriana fell asleep and dreamed fitfully of Scotty, trapped somehow in the case with the blue-winged specimens.

Their Thanksgiving meal was light but festive and Beatrice seemed almost happy as she spoke of the new condo she'd bought in Florida and her plans for the future. She had friends there—she'd made many when Uncle Robert whiled away the hours in the bar. "As if I needed more seashells!" she said, laughing.

They washed and dried the dishes, and since they were in the kitchen, decided to begin there. "You must take the crystal, Adriana, and share it with Tony, as it belonged to your grandmother and is the only thing we brought when we sailed for America. It's Venetian, very old." Adriana held a glass to the light and twirled it lightly. She knew without a doubt that she'd give it all to Felicia and Tony.

They spent the next two days going through the house room by room. Now and then she chose a piece, mostly some small item—a book of old photographs, a leather-bound collection of Shakespeare's plays, a crystal vase. She chose them more for her aunt's benefit than her own. Beatrice seemed pleased with each selection, saying over and over, "Yes, I'd pick that if I were you."

How can she part with it? Adriana puzzled. All these things she's collected, the fine old house itself? Beatrice talked of Florida as though getting there as soon as possible was the only thing that mattered. Adriana thought of her mother in the frantic days before each move. The sisters were more alike than either had realized.

Adriana lingered over a Chippendale secretary and chose it over the old piano. "I don't blame you," Beatrice said. "The sound has always been terrible."

How could she say what she felt, that the furniture was all, somehow, in *too good* condition, as though it had sat all these years, like the butterfly collection in the attic, hidden from view, shut away from the light.

She looked then at Beatrice and again saw herself twenty years hence. Adriana knew she never wanted to face the day when she would scatter her belongings among strangers.

Tony, Jr., and Licia would have their own homes. They wouldn't want her collections. Beatrice's house, despite all her treasures, was sterile. No one had ever loved in it, or created anything in it out of love. She was losing Scotty, and perhaps she had already lost the few remaining days they had, but that did not mean she had to marry someone like Calvin, or live a life centered on accumulation.

Adriana stopped in Wilkes-Barre and tried to call Calvin to apologize for missing Thanksgiving dinner. But Calvin's Utica phone was busy and there was no answer on the Syracuse line. She knew she should have called from Washington.

She'd known when she woke up at 9:00 a.m. that she'd never go to Syracuse or anywhere again with Calvin. In no time it was after one, yet Beatrice had continued to press item after item upon her. At last the ringing phone had given Adriana a chance to flee. She hugged her aunt and squeezed herself into the bulging car.

In her rearview mirror Adriana had caught sight of Beatrice, waving from the doorstep, beckoning her back, but she could not bear to accept even one more item. Anyway, perhaps Tony or Felicia could drive down before the sale.

But now, as Adriana tried the Syracuse number one last time, she wondered if the call her aunt had gone to answer had been for her. Perhaps Calvin had called to see if she'd left? What did it matter? If she had let them, Calvin and his mother would have planned the rest of her life for her. They might as well know now that it was over. She'd turn in her thesis, continue to teach and write, watch Biscuit grow. And she would try to find a way to say goodbye to Haines Scott.

She stopped for a late supper at a restaurant off the highway. Too tired to order from the menu, she asked for a quick sandwich. When the bacon, lettuce and tomato sandwich was placed before her, Adriana found herself remembering that first lunch Scotty had made for her.

One memory led to another, then finally settled into longing. It hurt. And giving him up would hurt infinitely more. But at least she knew now what loving was. If Scotty left...*when* Scotty left...perhaps then her heart would start to heal.

Two booths down, the elderly couple whispered and turned her direction. Adriana looked quickly away. The dark window beside her booth mirrored her tear-streaked reflection. Hurriedly she pushed away the half-eaten sandwich, paid the bill and pressed on toward home.

The nearer Adriana got to Rome, the deeper the longing in her heart seemed to grow. For all she knew, Scotty would be gone already, before she'd had a chance to thank him for at least opening her eyes to loving.

James Street was deserted and seemed unusually dark. Adriana swerved to avoid a mound of dirty snow left by the plows. Had there been a power outage? Another storm?

As she crossed Linden Street and headed up her block, her heart skipped wildly and leaped for joy. Scotty's old red pickup was parked in front of her house. He hadn't left. There was still time to tell him again that she loved him.

Adriana hardly noticed the lingering smell of acrid smoke as she parked behind the truck and stepped out. She picked her way up the sidewalk in the darkness. What could have happened that all the streetlights were out?

He sat on the porch step, his head leaned back against the rail, so that Adriana knew he was dozing.

He's forgotten his key for sure this time, she thought, smiling to herself. What did it matter? She was home now. She'd let them both in. She wanted his arms around her this moment. Nothing else mattered. Then she saw the house.

It all crowded in upon her at once. The smell of smoke, the dark steetlights, the boards across the shattered oval of the front door and the bay windows... ugly, black, jagged panes of dead glass.

"No," she choked out the words, trying to rush by Scotty. "Not my house."

"Adriana, you can't go in." He grabbed her roughly, held her to him, pressed her head to his jacket to force her eyes away. "Don't look, babe, don't look," he said, his voice rough with incredible fatigue and concern.

She buried her face in his coat. It smelled of smoke and sweat and deep within, his own familiar smell. It was that that brought her to her senses. He cringed as she drew back to look at him. "Scotty, what's happened to your hand?"

"Nothing, really—just a little burn. I've gotten worse in the kitchen," he tried to joke. "Adriana," he said then, his voice breaking, "I'm so sorry."

"Oh, Scotty," she said between sobs, "what about all your work in the kitchen?"

"I've built lots of kitchens," he started to say, then covered his eyes. "Adriana, I should have pressed you about the wiring." He nodded toward the darkened area where the fire had started in the attic.

"Biscuit!" She sprang to her feet.

"Easy. He's asleep in the truck. I could have strangled him. He hid in the basement. I finally got him out through the old coal chute."

"Is that how you burned your hand?" she asked.

He looked at her a long moment. "No." He stood up and pulled her to the truck. Biscuit growled half-heartedly as he opened the door. From underneath his blanket, Scotty pulled a stack of papers. The top one was singed and streaked.

"My stories," she exclaimed. "Oh, Scotty, I'd never have thought to save them." She hugged him again, but hastily drew back when she realized she'd brushed his injured hand again. He laughed and pulled her close, his kiss hard enough to still her tangled emotions.

"Where do you want to go, Adriana?" he said at last. "Tony said you could stay with him, of course. And your neighbors on both sides offered. And then, there's this."

She opened the folded note and recognized Calvin's small cramped writing. "He wants me to come to Utica," she read absently. "He's disappointed I missed his mother's party."

"He told me to tell you he's 'saved' the cloisonné vases," Scotty said. Adriana heard Scotty struggle to keep his voice level. "He was so delighted," Scotty related. "He said it didn't matter that you were late because he'd been here to save the only really valuable thing you own. And he said to remind you that he was the one who'd made you raise your insurance coverage last year."

As Scotty finished speaking, Adriana crumpled the note in a tight little wad and dropped it in the gutter. She looked into Scotty's tired eyes a long moment, then laid the manuscript carefully on the seat beside

Biscuit. "Do you want me to drive, Scotty?" she asked in a level voice. "I'm taking you home."

She tried to read his troubled expression. "I'm okay," she said. "Don't worry."

Chapter Ten

Felicia? Yes, it's Adriana... yes, I know." She listened as Felicia poured out her sympathy. Then Tony got on the phone and cried, and Adriana felt her own tears begin again. She brushed them away, cleared her throat, began again. "No...I'm at Scotty's. Tony, I'm worried. I thought he was just tired. I barely got him home. But I... I think there's something wrong. He's very warm, and he seems disoriented."

"The rescue squad tried to get him to check in to the hospital overnight. The burn is minor, but he took in quite a lot of smoke, I think. He kept insisting he had to be there when you got home. He's one hell of a guy, Adriana..."

"I know," she answered quietly.

"Did he start the medication?"

"I didn't see him take anything."

"Check the truck. I put it on the dash. He wouldn't

leave even to go to the drugstore. Is there anything we can do?"

"I don't think so," she answered. "Maybe tomorrow you and Felicia could bring me my car. I have some clean clothes in it. Aunt Beatrice sends her love."

She waited for the dial tone, then tiredly rang Calvin's house in Utica. No answer. But then, Calvin usually slept through anything. She'd call in the morning. The sooner the better.

His eyes were wide open, glassy with the fever when she returned with the medicine. Obediently he swallowed the pills she gave him. He flinched as she bathed his burned hand. Small beads of perspiration formed on his brow.

"You can yell if you want to, Scotty," she said softly.

"Yell?" he said, his voice dull and distant. "I might wake up Mom. The doctor says she's got to rest, you know."

"Of course," Adriana assured him. The perplexing words left an unsettling feeling before she could dismiss them.

He closed his eyes as she bathed his face and did not protest as she removed his shirt. Droplets of the cool water from her basin clung to the tangled coppery hair of his chest, where it disappeared in a tantalizing line below his belt.

Her fingers trembling, Adriana undid the buckle, loosened it, then pulled off his slacks and shorts. Quickly she covered him with sheets and blankets. Scotty opened his eyes then, focusing somewhere above her head.

"Adriana, are you there? Don't go. Please. I...I need you to hold the molding while I nail it... I need you."

She tried to catch and hold his fevered eyes, tears forming in her own. "I need you, too, Scotty." She choked out the words. Then she felt his grip on her wrist loosen as he fell into sleep.

She showered and found an old dress shirt of his to sleep in. For a moment she considered the couch downstairs. *I wouldn't hear him if he called,* she decided. She tiptoed to the bedside and stood over him. The copper-colored hair against the white pillow made her think of the monarchs her mother had pinned to the white cotton of the display case. Adriana crept quietly into bed and cradled this man she wanted to save from all entrapment, even her own.

He woke once, groaning. She rose and gave him more medication, wiped his hot forehead with a cool cloth until he slept soundly again.

She could not go back to sleep then, but lay staring into the darkness of the unfamiliar room.

She thought of the house, then. Her house, *their* house...gone. Salvageable perhaps, but she knew it would never be the same. Other hands would work on it, touch its secret places. The floors she'd sanded would need resanding, the countertop she'd touch would not be one that Scotty had touched. She turned on her side then and cried for what was gone and irreplaceable. And somewhere in the night, on the edge of her dreams, she felt the man beside her stir, turn, curve his body around her curled one. She thought of the folded wings of the monarchs, one upon the other, and slept at last.

Adriana awoke to the sound of the shower and the smell of fresh-brewed coffee. Across the empty bed beside her, the clock on the table read 9:00 a.m. She was calling the campus when he emerged from the shower. She pulled her eyes away from the towel tucked taut across his middle and tried to concentrate on the message she was leaving.

"You look a little more alive today," she said cheerfully. "Do I smell coffee?"

"Figured it was the least I could do," he said. "Here I'd planned to be the big hero, and then you ended up taking care of me." The grin she'd grown to love spread across his face. Adriana thought she'd never seen a sight so glorious. She bounded out of the bed to hug him, then colored at his appreciative glance. "Is this the new nurse's uniform?" he asked seductively. She darted back into bed and tried to cover her bare legs with one hand and button the half-open shirt with the other.

He smiled at her modesty, turned and pulled his own fresh clothes out of the bureau. "Tony and Felicia brought your car," he said, indicating the suitcase and makeup case beside the bedroom door. There was also a large box. Adriana recognized a label from one of the better stores.

"Looks like everyone was up early but me," she said. He looked at her a lengthy moment. She could not mistake the longing in his eyes. The hand that gripped the towel around his waist clinched tightly as he turned to go.

Adriana felt her breath stop as her longing rose to meet his own. She loved him, she *knew* it. And he loved her. But she did not want to try to hold him. Not *that* way. She shuddered as her breath escaped at last.

He was by her side in a moment, his arms cradling her. She could not stop the tears. They came pouring out of her like pent-up rivers released after a storm.

"I'll build you a new house, Adriana. I'll make them let me stay that long. We'll do it on the same lot, maybe salvage a part of the frame..."

She clung to him tightly, breathing deeply of the clean, damp smell of him. "It's just the starting over," she said, calm at last. "I don't know where to begin." She knew he could not guess half of what she meant.

"Tony and Felicia had the right idea," he said lightly. He left her side and returned with the box. Inside, Adriana found an assortment of clothing. Beautiful things, not just serviceable items. Felicia must have gone last evening and picked them out. Scotty tucked one finger beneath the clasp of a lovely lacy bra. "Why don't you start by trying on this to see if it fits," he teased.

She laughed, snatched up the bra and dashed for the bathroom. "Fresh towels are in the cabinet," he called. The lightness in his voice brought her back somehow. She wasn't sure of where they were, but they were definitely back.

Adriana stepped into the roomy shower and closed the glass door. She turned on the water full blast and soaped herself quickly, then let the spray pour over her. So the house was gone. So she'd start over. She'd had plenty of practice with that...

"Hello!" he called tentatively through the crack in the bathroom door. She turned off the water, cracked open the shower door and squinted across the steamy bathroom at Scotty. "Thought you might need shampoo," he said tentatively.

She laughed then, the sound of her voice ringing with joy off the tile walls. His laughter mingled with hers, adding resonance to the concert. Then, at practically the same moment, he loosened the towel and let it drop from his waist and she opened the shower door completely.

They stood for what seemed to her an eternity. She felt his eyes burn into her flesh, felt her throat grow warm with wanting him, felt her stomach tighten in its secret places. She stared at him and saw things she'd never seen. His cheekbone arching into that lofty look. The strong cords of his neck. The indentation below his ribs where the muscle stretched taut across his abdomen. And finally, the magnificence of his manhood. She closed her eyes against that sight.

He came in to her then, closing the frosted glass door of the shower behind him, wrapping them together in what seemed a spot secluded in space, a moment suspended in time.

He pulled her gently to him. She shuddered as the cool peaks of her erect nipples first brushed against his chest. Her body seemed all nerves as he touched her. Adriana seemed to feel more than his touch, more than his flesh against her own.

He drank drops of water from the hollow in her collarbone. Kissed her neck and then her ear so deeply that she shuddered with desire. She found his mouth and buried her own in it in one long, mindless kiss. His arms slid down her hips, pulling her close, impossibly closer, to himself.

Adriana felt her whole body begin to quiver with desire. It rolled in waves from somewhere deep inside and escaped in small cries that passed from her lips to his own. From deep within her own excitement, she felt him reach behind her and turn on warm water.

The tepid spray against her back lulled her, relaxing the outer excitement to move her beyond it. She felt the storm within her pass to something else, something deeper, fuller. A mighty roar rushed in her ears as though she'd been clasped, body and soul, to a giant seashell on some imagined strip of isolated seashore. Her body was no longer her own, and she knew that it was his to do with as he saw fit.

He led her back, farther into the shower, then turned her, her back to his chest, his hands cupped under her breasts, catching water, smoothing it up over her hardened nipples as if exploring them in an ocean of time. She felt the press of his thumbs as they caressed the swell of her breasts, felt herself warm in his palms with the water and his touch. Even the ridges of his fingerprints seemed discernable in the touch of his hand as he lifted her breasts to the warm stream of water.

Adriana arched her back to give him full access to her hardened nipples. The movement sent a shudder through his body that resonated in her own. His hands slid rhythmically down her abdomen, tangling in her secret places, fitting her hips against his own in a symphony of moves that seemed unrehearsed yet perfect. He lifted her slightly, slid his thighs under her for support. She leaned forward, bending, bending, until the water fell gently on the nape of her neck and she felt the intimate contact at last.

She could not tell if it started first in her or if her body simply sensed his own crescendo and matched it. She cried out first and his groan mingled in her own, then quiet filled the tiny room, except for the gentle sound of the water as it poured over them both and ran in rivulets down their joined bodies.

He washed her hair then. Wordlessly. She submitted to the massage of his fingertips in her scalp. Let him turn her, bend her, move her, this way and that, until her hair, her body, squeaked with cleanliness.

They stepped out of the shower together. Scotty threw open the bathroom window and sat down on the stool to dry his feet. She yelped with the rush of cold November air. He laughed and pulled her toward him, toweling her vigorously, ignoring her teasing pleas for warmth and gentleness. Something in his actions told her he was not finished with her yet, and she felt her nipples harden again in response to the thought.

He pulled her close to him, between his knees, and took the small, hard, dark rosebud of her nipple in his mouth, teasing it unmercifully with his tongue. He continued this until Adriana felt herself grow hot and moist again.

He held her lightly and she rocked against him, oblivious to the time, the place, to everything but his needs and her own and the one they had created between them.

At last he lifted her and set her gently on the bed. She curled into him and slept, full at last of loving him enough.

She told Calvin over lunch the next day and as she suspected, he was not surprised. He wanted her to keep the cloisonné vases but seemed relieved when she refused. In fact, he seemed relieved in general, and two days later she suspected why when she saw him lunching with one of the seniors from the writing clinic.

If only she could let go of the house as easily. She'd driven by it twice, but couldn't bear to stop. Each night she hurried home to Scotty. They'd cook together and he'd take her shopping and then they'd fall exhausted, but never too much so, into bed.

He called one night in mid-December to say he'd be a little late. "I'm going to pick up that contractor," he said slowly. Her heart skipped beats in the silence. Was he thinking again of leaving the air force, of staying in Rome? "I'm taking him to James Street, Adriana," he continued. "Rebuilding is not out of the question."

She murmured appreciation and waited for his "I love you...I'll be home soon, babe." Then for a long moment she sat on the edge of the bed and listened to the hollow empty sound of the dial tone droning in the gathering darkness of the early winter evening.

"Home?" Rome was her home, not Scotty's. She'd have to somehow kill the hope he'd stay behind, or it might destroy what little time they had left. She closed her eyes lightly against the image that rose, so frequently now, in her mind. She forced her thoughts away from rehearsing her goodbye. Always in her mind it carried her plea for him to stay and his own noncommittal answer.

She thought instead of the James Street house. The light streaming through the stained glass window in the dining room, through the oriel window in the east gable end of the attic, the etched oval glass in the living room door, and finally in through the wide bay window of the bedroom when she'd wakened that morning with Scotty beside her, his coppery hair bathed gold in the sunlight.

Adriana tried to touch each memory of the James Street house, as though to make it whole again. But the act was beyond her imagining, and she felt instead as she had when Aunt Beatrice had begged her to take her mother's furniture. No, she knew, it belonged to the past. Georgetown, James Street, all of it, was gone forever.

A sliver of moonlight spread out on the bed in Scotty's room. She stretched out her fingers to trace the quilt squares it illuminated. Curious combination, this ultramodern California house and the antiques they'd been collecting. And yet, it was home. Their home.

Why not stay here? She'd buy the house from Scotty with the insurance money. Somehow, living here, she'd be closer to him. He'd feel at home when he came to visit... If he came.

She lay back on the pillow and stared up into the high vaulted ceiling. Her eyes grew heavy and she slept. She dreamed first of a California valley filled with redwood houses with broad decks, and dogs and laughing children. And then she dreamed of a huge tornado that carried her away, in Scotty's house, like Dorothy in *The Wizard of Oz*. And finally she dreamed of the valley again and of herself in it.

She woke unsure of where she was, until the familiarity of Scotty's kiss and warm breath upon her half-open blouse brought her back. She held him tightly and would not even let him rise to undress and so they made love half-clothed, her skirt tangled around her waist, his belt hardly loosened.

"I've got a surprise for you," Scotty said later between bites of the hearty barley stew she'd fixed for dinner. He made her wait until he'd finished a second bowl of stew and then his salad, and the last of the burgundy. She drew the line at coffee and told him he'd have to tell his secret.

He made her dress warmly and took infinite care buttoning every last button of her parka. She was ready to scream with anticipation.

Finally he pushed her out the door and down the drive to where the truck sat parked in the snow. She watched, heartstruck, as he pulled the tarnished brass bed from the back of the truck and carried each piece carefully to the doorstep.

Adriana stood rooted to the ground, caught in the memory of the day they'd met, the butterfly autumn that had changed her life.

He hurried her into the house, all business now. They spread papers on the kitchen floor and laid out the bed. They worked for hours with brass polish and rags, cleaning smoky soot from every crevice of the frame. Finally they exchanged a look and a smile that said everything, and together they carried the bed upstairs.

When Scotty had finally lifted his own box springs and mattress onto the frame, Adriana felt surprised, somehow, that they fitted so well. She smoothed the quilt, lost in tangled thoughts of past, present, future coming together in ways now she could not understand.

The ringing phone interrupted her thoughts and forced reality to settle in around them. Scotty answered, as usual. It was still his house.

"Are you certain, Doctor? Did she leave any note this time? . . . Yes, I'll be there by midnight."

"It's my mother," he said. "She's . . . very ill. I've got to go to Denver."

"Of course," Adriana replied, searching his ashen face for the meaning he seemed unable to articulate. She helped him pack, wanting to ask questions but wanting also to respect his silence.

"It's likely to be a few days," he said. "You'll be okay?"

"Of course," she said. "I'll just miss you," she added tentatively.

He crushed her against him until she thought some fragile bone somewhere within her would snap in two. And then he was gone, the clank of the truck's loose fender echoing into the darkness.

Chapter Eleven

He'd been gone for two days when the telegram arrived. "Major Haines Scott. Urgent," the envelope read. It was from Edwards Air Force Base in California.

Adriana propped the yellow envelope on the kitchen table between the salt-and-pepper shakers and stared at it, letting her coffee grow cold in its cup. *Urgent.* They were always urgent. "Orders from headquarters," her father used to say lightly.

Beside her on the table, Scotty's notes from his last meeting with the contractor lay scattered where she'd been scanning them when the doorbell rang. Adriana pulled her eyes away from the black block letters on the telegram and focused on the fine, flowing script of Scotty's notes on the contractor's plans.

He'd become so intent on rebuilding the James Street house. Lately it had seemed as though he wanted to see it whole again even more than he wanted to see his own house finished. She felt at times as though he was afraid he would lose the thread of their time together unless he could see it taken up again in familiar surroundings.

And so he had made her promise to keep the appointment with the contractor. The doorbell rang for the second time that morning. Slowly Adriana rose to answer it.

"Off to California again, is he?" The older man shook Adriana's hand warmly, then settled himself at the kitchen table and bent over the plans.

"I see he's still intent on converting the garage to a guest house. Did he tell you about it?"

"He might have mentioned it," she said absently, "somewhere between the playroom for the attic and the workshop for the basement. Frankly I've been a little distracted..." Adriana ran her fingertips lightly over the top edge of the unopened telegram.

"Well, he has this idea that you need peace and quiet for your writing, so visitors should retire to their own quarters at a reasonable hour."

Adriana burst out laughing. *Peace and quiet for writing?* Why, she'd completely finished another story in the month she'd been with Scotty. Most of it had been written Saturday mornings when she'd awake early and reach for her tablet. The words would flow in rivers down the pages until the chilliness of the room forced her to snuggle down again and curve her shivering body around his warm one, seeking out the heat that grew more intense as he slowly stirred toward waking and wanting her.

Adriana felt her body warm at the thought of those moments. She felt a blush begin to burn its way up her cheeks, and so she lowered her eyes. "If Scotty thinks the garage should be a guest house, then I'm sure he knows what he's doing," she answered quietly.

There were other details to be covered, and Adriana felt weighed down by decisions. She didn't want to make choices without Scotty there beside her to help decide. The consultation was too blatant a reminder that she would live in the James Street house alone.

After the contractor had left, Adriana returned to the kitchen and cleared away the house plans. Only her coffee cup and the telegram remained. She did not want to touch it. Adriana raised her cup to her lips and sipped the coffee, oblivious to its cold and bitter taste.

She rose quickly and went to Scotty's desk in the living room where she knew he kept his address book. Mechanically she dialed Western Union and gave them Scotty's mother's address outside Denver. She would not open the envelope. Not unless he called and asked her to do it. Her hand remained poised on the receiver, almost expecting his call. Still, she started violently when the phone did ring.

"Adriana, it's Tony." The agitation in her brother's voice was intense. "Can you meet me at the airfield in an hour? Or sooner?"

"Of course, Tony, but what—"

"I can't explain now," he said. "Just be there. Please."

Adriana stood motionless until the soft click of the broken line merged into the droning dial tone. What was it in the sound of Tony's voice that seemed familiar? She carried her cup to the sink and stood a moment, staring out the kitchen window. The crystal clear sky was the color of blue ice, smooth enough to skate on . . . a perfect day for flying. *Flying?* It came back to her then, the memory of Tony's call to Scotty.

"Meet me at the airfield," he had said. It was the same tone, the same urgency. She'd gone skating that time; now she was the one who'd have to help him make the fragile moment count.

She brought the VW to a screeching halt just inches from the gate, jumped out and ran onto the small airfield. Beside the single engine plane, her brother stood hugging himself and shivering slightly, more, Adriana knew, from apprehension than from the cold. Scotty's friend Tom pulled the wooden blocks from beneath the plane's wheels. He stood and smiled and gave Adriana a half salute as she ran by him into Tony's arms.

"I want him to know I can do it on my own," Tony said. His voice sounded tight and yet resolved. "And I want you to know it, too."

"Me?" Adriana asked incredulously.

"It was the day the house burned, Adriana. You seemed to stop looking back. I knew I had to do the same. Scotty had been taking me up every day. When he left I thought I'd never make it. But yesterday I flew with Tom. I'm ready to solo. I'm going to do it today, Adriana. Now. And in February I'll be able to fly with Felicia and the children to Florida."

Adriana took off her scarf and wrapped it around her brother's neck. Tony swung himself into the cockpit and slammed the door. She shivered and backed away from the small plane as it began to warm its engine.

She knew that Tony was going over the takeoff checklist, item by agonizing item. She held her breath as she knew Tony must be also holding his. He taxied to the end of the runway and paused for only a moment. Then Tom gave a thumbs-up signal. The plane began to move down the runway, slowly at first, then faster and faster. Its nose rose slightly, then one wheel and then the other left the ground. Her brother, who feared flying above all else, was airborne. Tony was alone in the sky with his fear. But he'd learned at last, she knew, to live with it.

Adriana stood still, watching the plane rise and disappear into the horizon. Her heart rose with it. Wave upon wave of exuberance flowed over her.

Scotty. Look what he'd done for both of them. He'd given Tony his freedom. And her? He'd given her a part of himself that nothing could threaten, not fires or distance or . . . *moving*. The feeling swept over her slowly and deeply, bringing together the pieces of her life in a miracle of healing. She knew at that moment that home was inside her just as flying was inside Scotty. And she knew she would follow Haines Scott to the ends of the earth.

Adriana drove back to Lake Delta by way of James Street and stopped in front of the house. Snow had fallen on the walk and no one had bothered to shovel it. She set the engine in idle and parked for a while, remembering their time together in this house.

Scotty had shared that memory with her. He would share others. But leaving them behind was part of moving forward. Together they would build more houses, share more hopes, continue their dreams together.

He called the next evening while she was cooking. She heard his tired voice catch her excitement. "It's oxtail stew," she replied to his question.

"I can't believe this," he said. "You've learned to cook in three short days!"

"Oh, no," she replied. "It's just that I can *stand* to be in the kitchen now. Like Tony. Scotty, he's been flying."

"You're kidding, Adriana. It's wonderful! I had no idea he was ready—"

"Scotty," she interrupted, suddenly shy, trembling with what she was about to say. "Scotty, I'm ready, too."

"Ready for what, Adriana?" His voice took on a quiet, tired tone, and she faltered. She'd forgotten to ask about his mother.

"She's much better. She's out of the hospital now," he answered her question. "I've been doing some things around the house..." Scotty's voice drifted into vagueness. "I had a long talk with her doctor. He feels she'll be all right as long as she doesn't have to move. There's really nothing I can do. Let's talk about it later, okay?"

Adriana tried to absorb what Scotty was saying and to read what he held back. She could not sort out her thoughts before he began again. "I've received a telegram, Adriana," he said. The terrible distance she felt helpless to push back began flowing through his voice.

She tried to reassure him, tried to tell him not to worry. He hushed her as though he felt the line was too fragile to hold the trading of their innermost thoughts. "Just wait for me, Adriana," he said, the words somehow wrenching at her heart. "I have to go to Edwards for a couple of days. But I'll be back. Just wait for me."

She hung up the phone and stood a long moment in uneasy silence. Then, with an unsteady hand, she dialed Tony's number.

"It's just that I don't feel like being alone tonight," she said, her voice sounding small and troubled, even to herself.

"We'll be there in a flash," Felicia answered, but the warmth of her voice could not dispel the cold that clutched Adriana's heart.

"What do you mean, he's not accepting the California assignment?" The tension in her usual calm voice startled her brother, and Felicia looked up from her coffee with concern.

"Oh-oh, now I've done it," Tony muttered. "I guess it was supposed to be a surprise." Adriana registered the odd look that passed between her brother and sister-in-law.

"You must be mistaken," she said. "We settled that long ago. Scotty's a flyer. It's his life. I know now I can't ask him to change that."

"He knows you wouldn't, Adriana," she heard her brother say quietly.

"He called just before we left," Felicia answered. "He said he was glad Tony had conquered his fear of flying and he hoped to God he would be able to conquer his own love of it."

Adriana's thoughts raced wildly. He was giving up flying for her? But it wasn't necessary now. It was *wrong*.

"I never thought he'd turn it down, though," her brother was saying. "The chance of a lifetime."

"I think his mother's illness had a lot to do with it," Felicia added thoughtfully.

"Turn down what? What do you mean? What are you both talking about?"

"Didn't he tell you?" Tony asked incredulously. When she shook her head, he continued. "He finally made it. He'd been accepted for astronaut training at Edwards."

Astronaut training. His words came back to her. *To be the best at what you do.* She stared in astonishment as her brother continued. "He said he missed you too much, Adriana."

"Then why didn't he ask me to go?" she cried out.

"Maybe because he understands your need to stay put."

"No," said Felicia thoughtfully. "It was his mother's illness. The last time she got depressed and refused to eat, he was ready to give up flying and move back to Colorado."

Tony sighed and gave his own ample middle an affectionate pat. "One month in the pasta capital of central New York and she'll catch up in no time," he said. "Scotty should move his mother to Rome."

Adriana hardly heard the rest of the conversation. Her mind moved here and there among her memories of her time with Scotty, gathering pieces of the puzzle. *"My mother will be all right,"* she remembered him saying, *"as long as she doesn't have to move."*

So that was it. And she'd given him every reason to believe that she was the same way. Fragile. Afraid of change. How could she ever convince him that she was strong enough to stand beside him while he lived out his dream?

Adriana took the stairs two at a time. She pulled her suitcase out of the closet, struggled with the lock and then began tossing things into it at random.

Tony and Felicia followed. "Is this my sister who never makes snap decisions? Who never moves quickly?"

"This is your sister who's in love," Felicia answered. "Sit down and calm yourself, Adriana. I'll finish the packing."

"Will you keep Biscuit?" Adriana asked. "I'm going to California."

"So we gathered," they chorused.

Chapter Twelve

"We haven't seen him yet, Miss Anderson," the receptionist answered her inquiry. "He called to say he was flying to Pacific Grove first."

"Pacific Grove?" Adriana steadied herself against the receptionist's desk.

"He said something about butterflies. Said he had waited a long time for our decision; now we could wait for his."

Adriana felt her head begin to spin. *What had she done to him?* Was Scotty purposely trying to ruin his chances, hoping that the opportunity would somehow go to someone else because he had failed to report on time? And where was Pacific Grove? How would she ever find him now? Tears gathered suddenly and she could not stop them from spilling over.

The concerned receptionist insisted that she see the base commander.

"It's just the strain of flying all night," Adriana tried to tell him.

"Sit down," the commander urged gently. He was an older man with a thick crop of silvery hair and penetrating but thoughtful blue eyes. Adriana liked him immediately.

The commander tipped back his chair and threaded his fingers behind his head. "Haines Scott has not changed one iota since his days at the Air Force Academy," he said. Then he chuckled under his breath. "I'll never forget the day he walked out of my Introduction to Aeronautics class, just because he didn't want to miss the sunset. If Scotty has gone to Pacific Grove to see butterflies, you can bet it's a trip worth taking."

Adriana felt relief sweep over her. Her smile came spontaneously.

The commander picked up the phone, made a quick call and hung up. "If you are here to see Haines Scott," he said to Adriana, "I think we'd better find him for you. I don't think he'd ever forgive us if we didn't."

The receptionist entered with a slip of paper and passed it to the commander. He glanced briefly at the note. "Ask for Stan at the Aero Club," he said. "He'll know where to find Scotty."

Adriana clasped the outstretched hand warmly. Scotty was going to be in good company, she decided, if she could just convince him that it would not mean a choice between his career and her love.

"It's up near Monterey, Miss Anderson. It's a beautiful spot. I'm flying there this afternoon to pick him up. Would you like to come along?"

Adriana nodded tiredly. *I've come this far,* she thought. *I've got to let Scotty know that I can follow him anywhere.*

"Scotty always stays with me," Stan continued. "Why don't you let me drop you off at my place? You obviously need to rest. I'll pick you up later this afternoon."

Gratefully Adriana allowed herself to be tucked into Stan's station wagon. She leaned back and closed her eyes against the intense morning sun. The young man chattered amicably on . . . something about knowing Scotty for years. In a moment she was sound asleep.

The jolt of the car as it bounced onto a gravel road awoke Adriana abruptly. "Sorry," Stan said. "We're almost there. You really are beat."

Adriana smiled an apology and turned to look out the window. Desert landscape sped by on both sides of the car. The land was barren, but somehow clean looking. Together with the expanse of blue sky, it made her feel a sense of freshness and new possibility.

Stan slowed the car and pulled it into the circle drive of a low adobe house, its red tile roof glowing warmly in the morning sunlight. On either side of the front door, ocotillo cactus stretched inviting tendrils toward the creamy colored walls.

The moment she stepped into the terrazzo entry hall, Adriana knew that she was in another one of Scotty's houses.

"He did it the summer after graduation," Stan confirmed. "Solar energy was just getting off the ground, and Scotty wanted to experiment. I helped, but that only meant going into Lancaster for more nails and beer."

Adriana smiled. She could almost picture the situation. "It's his house through and through," Stan continued. "Now he's got to decide what to do with it when I leave for Germany next week."

Adriana stood in the long living room, bathed in sunlight from a south-facing glass wall that seemed to blur the distinction between indoors and out. Tentatively she touched the stone fireplace, its face already soaking up sunlight to warm the room once evening fell. Across one end of the living room, floor-to-ceiling bookshelves lined the wall. Adriana wandered over to them and found a library of books on houses.

"His father's collection," Stan supplied. Scotty had so much of his father in him, she mused. Perhaps that's why he feared that she was too much like his mother.

Stan brought in her bag and showed her down the hall to a bed-sitting room at the end. "Scotty sleeps here," he said. "I'm sure you'll be comfortable. Try to get some rest and I'll see you this afternoon."

Like the living room, most of one wall of the bedroom was glass, including a one-way window in the bathroom where a huge, emerald-colored sunken tub looked out over the empty desert and gave the illusion of an outdoor swimming pool. Adriana ran water into the tub, removed her clothes and slipped into the luxurious warmth.

Beyond the one-way window nothing stirred. The sun seemed to reflect off the sandy terrain like light bouncing off the facets of scattered diamonds. Here and there barrel, ocotillo and sagurao cactus dotted the landscape. Adriana slid down into the warm water until the purple mountains in the distance merged into a long, blue horizon. She felt like Cleopatra bathing in the Nile.

She was toweling off when she saw the jets. Like twin phantoms from some science fiction movie, they sped noiselessly far out on the horizon, so low to the ground that Adriana caught her breath. Then one plane dipped and turned and spiraled toward the upper atmosphere. The other followed suit as both planes soared at incredible speed, only a hairsbreadth apart, wing nearly touching wing. Then, just as suddenly, they seemed literally to fall out of the sky.

As the two planes tore along the horizon, Adriana felt a tremor begin in her belly and travel through her body. It caught in her chest and filled her until she wanted to cry out. This was Scotty's world, this atmosphere of speed and motion and power. He carried it with him always, even, she knew, into his lovemaking. The whole house was filled with it, and with him.

And he had the right idea about houses. It wasn't so much what you got from a place that made it your own, but what you gave. How would she ever explain that she, who had been so secure in only familiar surroundings, now felt freedom in knowing that any house, any place they shared, would be her home?

Wearily Adriana slipped between the sheets and closed her eyes. Again she dreamed the dream she'd had in Rome, of being swept away in Scotty's house, like Dorothy in *The Wizard of Oz*, and put down gently in a peaceful California valley.

When the plane took off at 4:00 p.m., it seemed to be chasing the sun, traveling up a long ribbon of gold as it stretched up the valley. Then Stan swung west and crossed the coastal range and Adriana caught her first view of the Pacific as it spread out before them, blue and flat and endless. Still, with every mile they traveled, Adriana felt a sense of comfortable familiarity with it all.

She'd seen them as soon as the small plane had landed. All along the runway, the butterflies rose, then rested, in the tall grass. The burnished gold, black-framed wing of the monarch was unmistakable.

"They winter here," Stan told her. "It's their west coast home." Adriana knew then why Scotty had come.

She left Stan at the coffee shop and crossed the road to the park in the forest of eucalyptus trees, hung thickly with trailing Spanish moss. The rich musty smell engulfed her, wrapping her in its heady scent.

The butterflies were there, huge clusters of them, wings folded against the gathering coolness of the evening, only their pale underwing color visible from where she stood. Adriana felt her whole life fold back upon itself, back to its true awakening, to that day she'd first seen sleeping butterflies with Scotty.

"Adriana!" She heard him shout her name.

A cluster of butterflies took startled flight. Spreading their golden wings toward the fading light, they rose in a crescendo of color that engulfed them both.

"Adriana," he said again when he reached her, crushing her against his chest, his voice husky, his breath warm in her ear. "You didn't have to come, Adriana," he said gently. "I was practically on my way...home. Oh, babe, did you miss me that much?"

She wanted to answer. She kept searching for words. But he kept supplying his own. Tender, sweet words that promised her all his love, security, marriage, all she had ever thought she wanted. "I'll never leave you again, Adriana. Just wait till you hear. I have... wonderful news."

His voice sounded heavy, tired in a way that she knew had nothing to do with needing sleep. Adriana knew she would have to begin to try to explain immediately. She could hold him this way for a while, but in the end, neither of them would be happy.

"Scotty, I..."

"Hush love," he said, still holding her. "Let's save it for later."

Scotty helped Adriana into the back seat of the small plane and fastened her seat belt securely. Stan sat up front to navigate, and Scotty swung himself into the pilot's seat.

There was something incredibly sensual in the way he put on and adjusted the headset, radioed for permission to take off and then maneuvered out onto the runway. It seemed as though the sky, the plane and everything it contained, including herself, were at his command. She watched his hands slide expertly over the controls, pausing deliberately at various positions as Stan called off items on the takeoff checklist. Scotty seemed to be fine tuning the aircraft, preparing it for takeoff, just as he fine tuned her body, preparing it for lovemaking. He'd drive this plane, jets and someday a spaceship, just as, she knew without question, he would soon be driving her to ecstasy.

The dull drone of the plane's small engine lulled her, and she slept, feeling as safe in Scotty's plane as she'd always felt in his arms.

She awoke only when the plane's wheels tentatively brushed the firm surface of Edwards' airstrip, then settled confidently onto the pavement and sped to a stop at the far end of the runway.

"We're home, Adriana," Scotty whispered, brushing her sleep-softened cheek with the back of his hand.

Home, she thought dreamily. He'd said it so lightly. Perhaps deep down he knew also that home was anywhere on earth they'd be together.

Stan tossed Scotty the keys to the station wagon. "I'm pulling night shift," he said. "I'll tie her down before I go. Why don't you take this lady home and feed her?"

Adriana inhaled deeply and leaned close to Scotty. The desert air was cool, dry and pungent. And it was fertile-smelling somehow in a way she could not find words to describe.

Adriana thought she saw Scotty's fingers tremble as he reached to fit the key into the lock of the house. Inside, she again tried to tell him, but his mouth covered hers and the first syllables of her explanation were lost in the depth of his kiss. She wanted to hold back, to change the subject. But she found that to be far more difficult to do when the mode of communication was physical, not verbal. Scotty had chosen the topic and the method.

As he deepened the kiss, Adriana felt her every thought turn to sensation. The feel of his lips on hers was soft yet demanding. His tongue probed gently yet firmly, forcing her to yield to its explorations. Even her fingertips felt sensitive to the finest strands of his hair as she tangled them in the copper-gold mass.

Suddenly he swept her up in his arms and carried her to the bedroom. Cradled against his chest, she could feel Scotty's heart beating in heavy, rapid rhythms that nearly matched her own. He placed her gently on the bed and undressed her slowly, kissing each inch of her skin as it was revealed to him. Then he stood to unbutton his own shirt.

Across the room, the window remained undraped, and Adriana looked out onto a world of quiet, blanketed by a sky filled with innumerable stars. It seemed as though the diamondlike sparkle of the desert sand by day had traveled to the sky to light the night. In the distance one star, a jet, moved across the horizon. Suddenly Adriana felt calm . . . and resolved.

She put her hands on his, where they reached to loosen his belt, and stilled them. She looked into his questioning eyes and felt a sort of unspoken pleading rise up inside her and settle in her own eyes.

"What is it, babe?" he asked softly. He sat beside her on the bed, cradling her in his arms. And Adriana cried. Where did these tears come from? she wondered.

"It's okay," he was saying. "Tomorrow we'll be back in Rome."

No, she thought. *Don't love me that much Scotty, not more than living.*

He wrapped her in his old velour robe and she buried her face in its burgundy folds, inhaling deeply the scent of his after-shave. Then he made her sit on the couch in the living room, a blanket tucked in around her, while he built a mesquite fire in the stone fireplace.

Scotty tossed potatoes wrapped in foil on the fire to bake and later spread two thick steaks on the portable grill. And after they had eaten, he poured her a glass of wine, and Adriana thought she'd never sipped anything so clean and pure and sweet. Then she began.

"It's the first time I've refused you," she said quietly. Her voice was low but stronger than she thought possible. The words seemed to roll like distant thunder from her heart.

He was crouched over the fire, prodding loose a fiery bit of mesquite. She watched the muscles in his bare back tense slightly as she spoke. When he turned, the light from the fire seemed to smolder in his brown gold eyes.

"The night's not over yet, my love," he said simply. A tone of confidence rang in his voice and Adriana shivered.

"But don't you want to know why?" she persevered.

"I think I know," he said, his voice taking on the protective tone that had comforted her so often in the past. Tonight it made her want to scream.

"No, Scotty!" Adriana nearly shouted the words. Then she was on her feet before him, both hands caught up in her wild, flowing hair, as if to drive the thought from her mind. She felt heat rise to her cheeks and color them to match the fire. She lifted her face to him, trying to stretch herself to match his height. And she felt, somehow, for the first time in their relationship, as sure, as strong, as confident, as she knew he felt. They were equals at this moment, and Adriana felt their love expand and fill the room with mutual protectiveness.

"What is it, Adriana?" he said. At last she saw that he was listening, waiting, not knowing, and knowing he did not know, but open and ready to accept.

"I will not have you give me everything, Scotty. Not now. Not ever. Not the part of you that needs to fly."

He parted his lips to protest, but she hurried on. "Somewhere in my life I stopped looking forward and tried to cling to what I already had. I thought that I could stay in Rome and stop the clock, keep things, and even people, frozen in time, a pond of memories where I could skate whenever I pleased. But Tony's learned to fly and Licia and Tony, Jr., will grow up. They can't be my weekend children forever. Life won't stand still while I play house, pretending there's no change, no risk, no tomorrow that may be hard to face. And I won't trap you there with me, Scotty. Home can be here, this house...or wherever we choose."

She watched his lips form a firm, tight line. "It's no life for a woman, Adriana. Look what it did to my mother."

"No," she said firmly. "Scotty, don't you see? She probably *needs* to move, to change, to be close to you and to your children... Scotty, even butterflies have to fly south in the winter or they die."

She spoke more softly now. "It wasn't all the moving around that made your mother doubt herself, Scotty, but losing your father, and knowing that if she'd moved *with* him, instead of *because of* him, she'd have richer memories, now that he's gone."

"That's not enough for you, Adriana," Scotty broke in. "I know you. You're a rooted person. I can't pull you up from everything you've grown to love, not just for the sake of richer memories."

He was almost shouting himself now. It was almost more than she could bear, but she stood her ground. "I'm not sending you up to the stars in that fragile bit of tinfoil, Haines Scott—and *you are going*—until I've made enough memories with you to last a lifetime. Here, now, and wherever else we are."

With those words still burning on her lips, Adriana tilted her chin defiantly and shook out her long auburn hair. Then she slowly loosened the robe and dropped it from her shoulders. It fell in a heap at her feet and she stepped out of it toward Scotty.

"Now, Scotty," she said simply. "Forever. Let it begin now."

She loosened his belt and then his clothes, too, fell in a heap with hers. They stood, hands clasped, with nothing but the light of the fire between them.

"I love you, Adriana," he said. "What I feel for flying will pass eventually. I know that now. It began somewhere in my childhood, and it will end, I know, somewhere on the other side of getting to the stars. But what I feel for you will last forever, wherever we are. That's the difference."

He drew her to him, smoothing her hair down her back. "I want other things now, Adriana, even more than flying. I want our children to ice-skate and toboggan and chase butterflies, if only for a while. I want them to know Tony. I want my mother to be there, too, and know you. And once I get this trip out of my system..."

"However long it takes," she murmured, then hushed his response with her kiss.

When at last they drew apart, Adriana saw her reflection held securely, lovingly, in Scotty's eyes, just as she knew her own eyes held the vision of the man she loved. Wordlessly they dropped together onto the thick carpet in front of the fire.

Suddenly the fire glowed golden. A burst of tiny sparks traveled up the chimney like a mass of monarch butterflies suddenly set free. And in that moment Adriana felt her spirit soar, with Scotty, somewhere toward the stars.